THE MYSTERIUM

THE MYSTERIUM

ERIC MCCORMACK

St. Martin's Press
New York

Library of Congress Cataloging-in-Publication Data

McCormack, Eric P.
The mysterium / Eric McCormack.
p.   cm.
ISBN 0-312-11320-X
1. Journalists—Fiction.   I. Title.
PR9199.3.M42378M97   1994
813'.54—dc20   94-19653   CIP

First published in Canada by the Penguin Group

First U.S. Edition: November 1994
10 9 8 7 6 5 4 3 2 1

For Nancy, Michael and Jody

THE MYSTERIUM

1

There has to be a point where the journeys of forgetting stop and the forms remember.

W.S. MERWIN

You who read this, don't be afraid. Bend over the book carefully till your nose is no more than a half-inch from the pages. Inhale. Inhale again. Do you smell coal smoke, and traces of dead bracken and heather, and any other scents a north-east wind carries on a March day in the northern part of this Island? Do you smell, mixed in with them, a hint of something strange, something unlike any smell you've ever encountered before?

You do? Good. You're probably still safe.

But you who smell nothing but the paper and the binding — a whiff of cheesecloth, sizing, glue, printer's ink, the leather of the cover; you, in short, who smell only a book, beware. For you it may already be too late.

In my own case, I trace the beginnings to an official banquet and a quiet policeman — a Reeve, from the South. At that time I was still a student, and worked in my spare time as a sort of apprentice reporter for *The City Voice*. All my copy had to be submitted to the city-desk editor whose only axiom was that my stories should be no less dull than the events I reported on. That was easy enough — I covered City Council meetings as well as its sub-groups like the Committee on Utilities and Suburban Sewage or the Committee for Re-carpeting Administration Buildings (CUSS and CRAB I would like to have called them in my reports).

It was at midday on the second Friday of April that year that my apprenticeship took a strange direction. I think I can safely use that expression. I was sitting at my desk at *The Voice*, staring out the window, as I often did, across the street to the Necropolis (an elegant name for the graveyard here in the Capital). It had long ago dawned on me that few if any of the varied and wonderful stories that appeared daily in *The Voice* would endure as long as the forgotten names and the forgettable messages sculpted on those gravestones.

At any rate, I was sitting at that desk on that day when the phone rang.

"James Maxwell? This is Reeve Blair. We met a couple of months ago at the banquet."

I remembered (I used to place great trust in my own memory then) both the banquet — the Civic Awards Banquet — and the man: a tall policeman, a Reeve from the south of the Island. He sat beside me at a corner table out of the direct line of fire of the corporate speech-makers. He didn't have the air of some reeves, confident in their ability to persuade the weak to reveal themselves. Rather, I thought he might have been a monk, with his stoop, ascetic face, grey eyes, close-cropped greying hair to match and quiet southern voice. We chatted for a while and when I asked him about his profession, he said this:

"Some men join the force because they want to bring justice to the world, to make criminals pay for their crimes. Others, like me, enlist because we love a mystery. It's the challenge that attracts us."

I said nothing, but I was really quite surprised at such an idea.

"I also believe," said the Reeve, "that there are criminals who aren't so much interested in profiting from crime as in presenting mysteries for us to resolve."

Now, as I heard his voice again, I could picture Reeve Blair's face quite clearly, and I remembered how he spoke slightly out of the corner of his mouth. A strange quirk — his lips seemed to make a little noose around his words.

"I want to put a proposal to you," he was saying over the telephone. "I'd like to send you a document to read. After you've read it — if you're willing — come and spend a week here in Carrick."

"Carrick?"

"Yes, Carrick. That's where I'm calling from."

Even then, Carrick was in the news. Or perhaps I should say it was in the news for *not* being in the news. After the first few incidents there, everyone was aware only of the news blackout on the place and the area around it. The police and the military had cordoned Carrick off and we'd heard only rumours, mutterings about "plague," and "disaster." But no one really knew what was going on, no one really knew the truth (another one of those words that meant so much to me once).

I told the Reeve, certainly I'd agree to read the document, whatever it was.

"You'll find it very instructive." His voice was soft. "But you must promise not to disclose its contents to anyone else till I say it's all right."

I agreed to that too. I would have agreed to almost anything for the opportunity of finding out the facts about Carrick.

He said one last thing:

"At the banquet that night, James, you asked me what was the most unusual case I'd ever dealt with. This is it."

Funny. I remembered so many things about that night but not asking him that specific question, the one that changed my life.

Later on the afternoon of Reeve Blair's phone call, the document he'd promised arrived by military courier and I sat down at my desk and read it. And I read it again.

I once heard the curator of the National Museum talk about the challenge of trying to conjure up some ancient culture on the basis of a few shards of pottery, or of reconstructing some long-extinct monster from a fragment of bone, or even a claw. I think I understood that kind of perplexity on the day I read the document from Carrick.

I submit the text of it here, exactly as I received it.

THE DOCUMENT

My name is Robert Aiken, pharmacist at Carrick. My father, Alexander Aiken, was the pharmacist here before me.

4

Yesterday, Tuesday the 20th of March, at about three o'clock in the afternoon, I climbed the steep path till I stood on the cold, wet shoulder of the Cairn. The soldier with me was a young man who kept me covered with his rifle. For maybe the thousandth time in my life, I watched the valleys below thickening with fog like the lungs of a slow-breathing monster. To reach Carrick, the fog has to roll over range after range of hills. It wipes out the borders between countries and the lines between earth, sky, sea and shore.

Shepherds don't like such days: their sheep melt away like pictures returning to their negatives. And those days are dangerous for strangers on the high moor with its marshes and sudden deep ponds.

But for me, up there on the Cairn, the wind on my face was like a mother's kiss, even though it was a cold one. For an hour or two, at last, I was away from the afflictions in Carrick town. So I took pleasure in watching the way the fog moved in; till all I could see of Carrick was the steeple of the Church jutting out as though it were the sword of one of those drowning kings. Nearer, I could still make out a few trees, sparse as tombstones, and the whitewashed cottages of shepherds, and the tangled ropes of streams among the gorse.

Any scraps of colour that still remained at this late stage of the winter were also in the process of evaporating in the fog, like one of those elixirs my father taught me to make. He'd show me how to mix the red borage, the yellow saxifrage and the black bugloss into swirling colours. Then he'd allow me to add the thyme. Together we'd watch the compound slowly turn grey — grey as certain days on the Cairn.

"It's time to go back down, Aiken," my guard said.

He'd been watching my every move, afraid no doubt that I might perpetrate some last, awful deed. He flinched when I suddenly stretched out my arms to hug the faintly scribbled landscape. He had no need to worry; it was my farewell embrace. I knew I'd never stand there again.

TODAY, THURSDAY, I'M SITTING by the window of my living-room above the Carrick Pharmacy where I practise my trade. A late afternoon fog is slinking into the town. I once told the Colonial, Kirk (Kirk, of all people!), about the legend that in centuries past whole villages disappeared in such fogs, and failed to re-materialize after they lifted.

Kirk didn't laugh.

As for Anna, if she were sitting by me now she'd surely disagree with me on this matter of the fog's thickness; she always enjoyed our debates on the weather. For example, I might suggest to her that from my perspective here at the window, the buildings on the other side of the Green were barely managing to remain solid.

"That means this fog's going to be very thick," I might say.

"You're quite wrong, Robert Aiken," she might reply and point out that certain chimney stacks and certain doorways were still quite visible. She might draw my attention to the clarity of the writing on the sign outside The Stag. And so on.

Sadly, Anna and I will never play that game again —
or any other of our games. For one simple, unchallenge-
able reason. The buildings in Carrick still persist, tangible and solid in spite of the fog. But the people of Carrick,
Anna among them, are in the process of an irreversible
disappearing act.

They are all dead or dying.

As I look now out of the window, waiting for the great
clock of darkness to strike on this March day, I know
Carrick will soon be a ghost town. It contains practitioners of the various trades as it did in its heyday;
except that now they're no longer townspeople —
they're strangers.

I'm referring, of course, to the doctors and nurses who
descend day and night from the barracks to fuss with
the dying. Or to conduct test after test on me to find
out why I'm still alive and apparently well. I include
in their number the police from the Capital prowling
the town in cruisers the shape of giant black toads. And
the platoons of khaki-clad soldiers daily hammering
two-by-fours across the doors and windows of the abandoned buildings.

Though most of the soldiers are young — really only
apprentices, unsuited as yet to deal with the calamity
that has struck here. A week or two ago one of them said
this to me:

"Don't worry, friend. We're only here to guard against
looting. Until everything's settled."

I didn't ask him: Would any thief have the nerve to
enter such a remote, such an unlucky place as Carrick?

In the days that have passed since he said this, the soldiers have given up the attempt to draw me into conversation. I believe they now look at me in the manner of vipers whose eyes see only the red aura of the prey.

I must admit this reaction doesn't surprise me. Only those who are intimate with crime know that it's the same everywhere; that we who live in these little towns are no more guilty than the rest.

I sometimes think it's not individual human beings but this world we all inhabit that requires the death sentence.

KIRK. A LOT NEEDS TO BE SAID about Kirk, though I find it very hard to talk about him. I have to haul myself hand over hand along the insubstantial rope of days that leads back to the first time I saw him.

Early January, it was. He was standing in the street outside the Pharmacy, looking in the window at the display of the traditional tools of our trade (there's been a pharmacy in Carrick for centuries). I'm sure Kirk, like most other people, must have found the display interesting. On one side lie the researcher's implements: bowls and pestles, test tubes, bottles of every colour, Bunsen burners. On the other side are the surgeon's grim paraphernalia: forceps, trepanning saws, speculums, kidney basins, stomach pumps, germicidal lamps, syringes, lancets, swabs, probes.

My father, Alexander, was the collector of these objects. "We at least belong to the gentler part of the trade," he used to say.

I rarely close the curtain that separates the window from the inside of the store because my father, all through the period of my training, insisted that a pharmacy must give the impression of openness. Any passer-by must be able to look in and see everything: the equipment in the window; further back, the interior of the store; and us, the Aikens, father and son, behind the high counter mixing our compounds.

"Never be afraid to let them see us performing our mystery," he would say. Our mystery. When no one else was around he would use that ancient word for our ancient profession, and he would smile.

But, to return to the matter of Kirk. On the January day in question — Wednesday the tenth — I had looked out to see how the weather was. The sun was just visible behind the clouds like a concealed lamp illumining the sky up there, but leaving the earth below in murk.

I glanced out, as I say, but saw no one at the window. A minute later I glanced out again, and Kirk was standing there. I knew it must be Kirk. In these towns where everyone knows everyone else, any stranger is conspicuous. (Even in the old days, during the Festival, visitors were as much curiosities as were the performers.) So I'd heard from several townspeople that a man named Kirk — a Colonial — had taken a room at the The Stag. And here he was at my window.

He was about my own age and build: a wiry man in his mid-forties, middle height, with thick, greying hair. He wore brown cords and a heavy, green wool sweater. He was carrying a fishing-rod in his right hand; a black tin box was hanging from his left shoulder.

9

That was the Kirk I saw through my window. His blue eyes entangled with mine for a moment, then he turned and walked away. I didn't even have a chance to acknowledge him or to make myself smile at him.

I do remember certain other details: it was three o'clock exactly when he paused for a few seconds at the window of the Pharmacy, looked in, saw me, knew that I saw him, then turned and went away. Three o'clock. And another detail: I walked over to the window to watch where he was going, and right in front of my eyes in the corner of the glass I saw a fly, a winter fly, caught in a web, wringing its hands. I wiped away both the fly and the web with my sleeve.

For details like that to have impressed me so deeply, I must have instinctively understood how significant the moment was.

Kirk, by now, had crossed the street and entered the Green. He suited it that day. I mean, at some times of the year the Green looks so formal you feel you should be wearing a tie to cross it. But in January, with all those wilted stalks of last year's flowers protruding from the dead grass, Kirk's rough-and-ready clothes were quite correct. He carried his fishing-rod the way someone not used to fishing would carry one — as though it were less a fishing-rod than a divining-rod that was leading him somewhere. He followed it past the scattering of trees and benches to the Monument where he paused and looked up at its three figures. Then he went across the road and on past the Carrick Church.

The rod kept drawing him along towards The Stag. When he arrived there, he braced the door ajar and manoeuvred the end of the rod inside; then he himself lunged in after it as though he'd been hooked, as though he was more the prey than the predator.

IN THE WEEKS THAT PASSED AFTER my first glimpse of Kirk, Carrick was nothing but what it always was: a quiet town in the hills. The days went by dully. A mixture of cold rain and high winds atoned for the absence of snow. The fog, of course, was frequent — people who live in these hills easily understand how it must feel to be colour-blind.

Often in the mornings I'd deliver supplies of pills and various elixirs to other men of my trade in the pharmacies at Drumner and Lannock and Shiels. These towns are almost indistinguishable from Carrick, tethered together by sinuous roads. Just as my father did before me, I'd finish each morning's deliveries by stopping for lunch at the hotel in Stroven then drive back to Carrick.

As for the Colonial, Kirk, I knew that during those weeks he took daily hikes with his fishing-rod into the hills. Always he carried that black tin box. Some of the local fishermen said he pottered around at the streams, but visited only one fishing hole — the St Giles Pond, four miles east of the village.

No one had actually seen him fishing.

EVERYTHING CHANGED ON A FRIDAY morning, three weeks after I first saw Kirk.

The night had been windy — one of those winds that blows in from far away to the east and builds up its strength over the Northern Sea. It flattens the breakers in the Firth and ransacks the coastal villages and the farms. Then these Upland hills rear themselves against it and comb it into strands, making such a noise you'd swear the high valleys were flutes in an organ that wasn't tuned for human ears.

As a result, I didn't get to sleep till well after two, and when I did, I slept badly, harrowed by a bad dream. I dreamt I was in a large room with no furniture and no doors. The only other occupant of the room was a black-and-white collie. I was following him around, battering him with a gnarled walking stick, till his head and the stick were covered with blood. The dog's brown eyes looked so sad I struck harder and harder, hurling myself into each blow.

It was a relief to wake up. On nights like that, sleep is a wound and waking is the bandage around it.

I hadn't been awake long when I heard a rapping at the window downstairs. Then: "Robert! Robert Aiken!" someone shouted. I found my slippers and went down into the chill of the Pharmacy. It was Cameron who was calling my name. He was peering through the window, his hands bracketing his face like a diving mask against the gloom.

I opened the door.

"Come and look," Cameron said. He was wearing his brown shop coat. He's the Carrick baker, a calm man with a round face. He was pointing towards the Monument where I could see a number of townspeople gathered. It was raining lightly, and there was no sign of fog.

"What's the time?" I asked.

"Late enough," he said.

I put my oilskin coat over my pyjamas and followed him onto the Green. The night wind had disappeared. I could hear my own breathing and see it tromboning out before me.

The villagers standing at the Monument were silent. Some of them turned and nodded to me: Miss Balfour, in her hooded yellow rain-coat; Doctor Rankin, his black greatcoat and black bowler glistening. And Anna. She was wearing a shawl over her shoulders and was bare headed. Sentinel Hogg was stooped in front of the Monument, his broad rump straining at his pants.

This Carrick Monument is typical of its kind. It has a marble plinth, two life-size soldiers made of lead in battle dress, leaning forward with their bayonets at the ready, protecting a female lead figure — Liberty — in a flimsy robe. All three of the figures stare at something ahead.

The children of Carrick (when there *were* children in Carrick) used to wonder what it was the three were looking at. At some enemy only they could see? At the disused Carrick Church directly in front of them? At the hills beyond? Long ago, I made myself intimate with the sharp edges of the plinth and the textured coldness of the figures. Along with the other Carrick boys I used to climb the Monument, caress the groin and the exposed nipples of Liberty and look directly into her face and the faces of the two guardians.

That was how we found the answer to the mystery. The eyes of the three figures were carved inwards, looking back into themselves. The enemy was an enemy within.

But the mystery of the eyes wouldn't tease anyone any longer. On that January morning, all of us gathered there on the Green could see that the lead faces of the three figures had been hacked away and only ridged scars remained. Further down, jammed into the groin of Liberty, was a bayonet that had been broken off one of her guardians' rifles.

Sentinel Hogg, his eyelashes fluttering rapidly as they always do, was looking for clues in the manner of his trade. He was most anxious about the plinth, where there should have been a metal plaque with the names of all townspeople killed in the War. For there was no plaque now, only an indecent blank space, like exposed white flesh; and on the space, sprayed in red paint, was a large circle.

The townspeople were muttering, "disgraceful" and "shocking" and "unbelievable." Miss Balfour and Doctor Rankin looked over at me and shook their heads. Anna kept staring at the Monument. The chill was penetrating my oilskin, and my feet were cold. I felt myself begin to shiver, so I turned away and walked back across the dead grass to the Pharmacy.

DID I SUGGEST EARLIER THAT nothing extraordinary happened for several weeks after my first sight of the Colonial, Kirk?

That's not quite the case. I might have mentioned my first actual meeting and my first conversation with Kirk. It took place on a Saturday night just a few days after I saw him outside the Pharmacy window.

On that Saturday, around six in the evening, I hung

up my cloth coat, put on my raincoat, switched off the lights and stepped out into the fog. I walked east, past the darkened EzeShop grocery and past Thomson's Men's Tailor; the plastic dummies in his window were naked under brown paper for the weekend.

Anna's store is next to Thomson's at the junction of the street and a lane that runs north. Her entrance is angled across the corner. The sign above it in gothic letters reads: ANTIQUES.

As I passed her street window I noticed in it some of the objects I had seen so often before: a lacquered table with short bow-legs; and standing on top of it a stuffed white dog, also bow-legged. The dog had a black patch on its chest in the shape of a heart or some familiar land mass, depending on how you looked at it. Behind the dog a clutter of dented spittoons and brass ornaments almost blocked the view of a wall map of what was once an empire — its territories were now a faded pink colour.

When I pulled open the heavy wooden door, the brass skull with the clapper inside jangled from the lintel. I stepped inside and shut the door.

Anna wasn't in the store but I could hear the creak of the floorboards in her rooms above. As I walked along the centre aisle, I took careful note of how she'd arranged the objects in the store that day, for I like to believe it's possible to gauge the minds of the practitioners of some trades by the way they set out their wares. Especially I noted: the old desk with dozens of tempting nooks and crannies; an ancient radio with a dial depicting the cosmos; a sheaf of assegais and leather shields from some old war; brown portraits of a sad woman; paintings of huddled northern hills and grey lakes; leather albums full of sepia photos of families long dead — even the plump babies; faded naval uniforms on headless dummies; spiked duelling pistols; sets of bagpipes with rips in the bags; skean-dhus and dirks; plaid bonnets; and books, books, books.

Some objects I didn't linger over: for example, the brocaded chairs, lavabo jugs and basins, tarnished cutlery, Tiffany lamps and dwarf porcelain elephants. I always suspected such items were put there by Anna simply to mislead.

On this particular Saturday I saw she'd laid out her glass box of giant moths and her case of varnished autumn leaves from the northern forests. "What does it mean, Robert Aiken, that people love to see nature in the throes of death?" So she'd asked me when she first came into possession of these moths and leaves.

I could also see, plainly displayed, two pairs of stuffed pheasants and a huge salmon. "If we're all descended from fish and birds, does that mean hunting and fishing are nothing but permissible forms of murder followed by cannibalism?" She'd wanted my opinion on that.

Now I made my way along the worn bamboo runner-mat that dissects the floor and disappears under the blue curtain in front of the stairs. A table that's shabby but not antique stands in front of the curtain. A pile of papers, a receipt pad, ball-point pens and a wooden cash-box always lie on the table. Faint traces of Anna's perfume are in the air in that part of the store.

I could hear her footsteps now descending the stairs. At the bottom, she stopped for a moment.

The curtain swished aside and Anna stood revealed, fair haired and pale of face.

She looked at me mysteriously. I made sure I didn't smile, for she loves little pieces of theatrics like this entrance. She was wearing a long, green skirt and a green sweater that matched her eyes.

"It's you, Robert Aiken." Her voice has a certain brittleness, or maybe fragility's a better word. Her voice is as fragile as a rare vase.

"I've had a good look around," I said. "I think I've guessed the theme for today."

She looked around too and smiled just a little, something she rarely does, as though it's a breach of some etiquette she alone observes.

"Dissolution," I said. "The theme is dissolution."

"Your appraisal says more about you, Robert Aiken, than about my display."

"Perhaps. When I'm hungry, my mind isn't as sharp as it might be. I just dropped by to invite you to dinner at The Stag. Interested?"

She was. She said she must go for her coat. She went back through the curtain and I heard her ascend that familiar, dark staircase.

ANNA AND I WENT OUT INTO the evening. The street lamps had linked their arms feebly against the fog and the night, and so did we. Instead of crossing the Green as we usually did, we walked round it past the Church from which no sound has emanated since the end of the War, and past the Library. We went into The Stag.

At the dim reception area to the left of the lobby, a huge rat was bent over gnawing at some papers. The rat looked up, miraculously transforming itself into Mitchell, the owner, at his bookkeeping.

"How nice to see you both," he said. "Dinner?"

He led us up the staircase with its faded wallpaper and paintings of dark landscapes, to the spongy landing. He opened the door of the dining-room; the wraiths of generations of long-dead cabbages greeted us.

No other guests were seated in the dining-room, a place of mahogany panels and low hanging lamps. Taped chamber music was playing. Three of the six tables were set for dinner. Mitchell took our coats and hung them on the octopus stand by the door then sat us at the window-table, our usual table, where we could look out over the Green. The fog was still light enough that through our reflections in the window we could see the Monument and the pine trees; but we could barely make out the Pharmacy on the far side or Anna's store. We could see nothing at all of the obscure sentences of the hills looming all around Carrick.

We drank some wine and ordered dinner. It was no more memorable than usual. Food at The Stag is so plain you might be eating a piece of the grey landscape. Indeed, I remember Anna saying to me once as we sat at that same table, "I wonder if we are what we see, as well as what we eat; if the sights we grow up with form us as much as the food we're reared on."

As always, we talked and ate. The rituals of the meal were as comfortable this night as ever. We'd finished and were just about to leave when the dining-room door swung open, and in walked Kirk.

His grey hair was combed and he was wearing a tweed jacket and a shirt and tie. He moved to a table near the door, the farthest from us, and eased himself awkwardly into a chair. His days of unaccustomed hiking had turned his legs to stilts.

Anna and I rose and made our way to the door. It was our custom after we ate at The Stag to go down to the bar for an after-dinner drink, away from that cabbagey aura. Anna often said it clung to her clothing for hours ("You think perhaps we are what we smell, too?" I used to ask her). As we passed Kirk's table, I stopped.

"Kirk, isn't it?" I spoke quietly, that first time, as though he were a man who might be offended by noise. "We're going downstairs to the bar for a drink. Why don't you join us when you're finished your meal?"

The blue eyes looked at me coolly and I thought he was going to refuse. But then he nodded.

"Sure. Why not." He didn't look at Anna. "I won't be long."

DOWN THE CREAKY STAIRCASE and through the lobby, Anna and I made our way. The clock over the reception desk said seven o'clock.

The bar is darker than the rest of The Stag. It holds another archaeological layer of smell — decades of pipe and cigarette smoke. Opaque windows prevent anyone outside from seeing the worn leather couches, the wooden tables and chairs. A series of framed pictures hang on the panelled walls; the eye gradually transforms

them into bleak landscapes someone might have pho-
tographed on a planet with no sun. At the far end of
the room, the ceiling above the big fireplace is black
with soot from a fire that burns, winter and summer. A
taped piano entertains merrily, even when there are no
customers.

We sat down.

"I hope you didn't mind that I asked Kirk down," I
said.

"Not at all," she said. "It'll be a change."

I made no comment on that. Mitchell came through
the door behind the bar and brought us our drinks. We
sipped slowly, and waited for our guest.

KIRK MUST HAVE DECLINED The Stag's special
bread-pudding dessert too, for he came in not long after
and sank in that stiff way beside Anna on the leather
couch. The springs sagged and their hips touched; but
Anna made no effort to move away from him. We introduced ourselves formally. His first name was Martin, he
said, but he preferred plain Kirk. Mitchell brought him
his drink and left us.

"You're on holiday?" Anna asked.

She was studying his face.

"Pleasure and business. A little bit of each." The nasal
accent of the Colony made the words sound exotic to us,
used as we were to the rough speech of Carrick. And he
spoke quite slowly, savouring the words where we would
have spat them out.

"I saw you the other day coming back from fishing,"
Anna said.

"Yes. But I'm no fisherman." He was answering her but he was looking at me, though I'd said nothing at all. I looked back at him, and his blue eyes didn't flinch. It was impossible to tell if they'd ever been bruised by intimacy.

"You said business, too?" Anna asked. She was asking all the right questions.

"I work with water. I study water in various parts of the world. I'm a hydrologist." He wasn't apologetic about the technical word.

I understood now the reason for the metal box I'd seen him carry — he was another tradesman in Carrick, carrying the tools of his trade.

"Isn't water just water, no matter where you go?" Anna asked.

"Water is no more constant than we are," he said without any hint of a smile.

The silence after that was rather uncomfortable, so I spoke for the first time.

"One thing about Carrick. There's never any shortage of water here. Is there Anna?"

"Really. Rain, rain, rain. Some years, it rains every day." She granted Kirk one of her rare smiles, and that seemed to encourage him.

"So you've both lived here all your lives? I'd like to know something about the history of Carrick. It would be useful for me when I'm analysing contaminants. For example the old wall that runs along the west side. Did it crumble away over time? Or was it dismantled? It looks to me as though parts of it have been deliberately vandalized."

He directed these questions at me, so I was obliged again to look straight into his eyes. In their depths it might have been ice I saw. I felt quite apprehensive.

"If you do a bit of travelling around the Island," I said, "you'll see that destroying things has been a pastime here for centuries. Maybe it's hard for Colonials to understand that."

"No, it's not hard. Not at all," he said, speaking directly to me. "Our early settlers all came from the Island. They liked the Colony but they must have thought the soil wasn't fertile enough. So they fertilized it with Indian blood. No records were kept, so for a long time that was one of the great mysteries in the Colony — where all the Indians went." His eyes gave no hint of irony. He kept looking at me. "What about Carrick though? Surely it has its mysteries."

I asked him what he meant.

"That old mine, for example," he said. "The one up beside the St Giles Pond. I'd like to know what happened up there. Why was the mine closed? When was it closed?"

The blue of his eyes was so clear it was impenetrable. I thought to myself: if he isn't a complete innocent, then he's a man with the best of disguises — the appearance of complete innocence. I had to choose my words carefully.

"I'm not a historian, I'm afraid." I hoped my voice sounded calm.

Again there was a silence, till Anna spoke. She changed the subject now, made sure we talked about less dangerous things — about Kirk's work, about the places he'd travelled. He seemed to relax a little, or perhaps it was we who relaxed. He became quite entertaining, it seemed to me, and began concentrating on Anna. He used his adventures to woo her; and I must admit he showed great mastery of the ritual advances and retreats.

When he'd finished his second drink, he stood up slowly and said he must be going — he'd an early rise.

"How long will you be staying in Carrick?" Anna asked.

"At least a couple of months. I hope I'll see more of you. And you too, Aiken." His legs were even stiffer as he left the bar.

Anna watched the door close behind him and kept watching as though she could see him go through the lobby and limp up the dark stair towards the guest rooms.

"What are you thinking, Robert Aiken?" she asked. "He seems to be a nice man. He seems friendly."

I was apprehensive about Kirk; but I knew she liked him. I wondered, as I always did when she took an interest in another man, if they could become the great two-headed animal, love.

"Yes, he seems to be," I said, adding another brick to her wall of seemings. "Time will tell."

Around ten, I walked her back to her store. It was raining now, a cold rain. And I was so sure the fog was much thicker than when we went to The Stag, I said so. She said I was wrong. At her door, she thanked me for the dinner and the drinks, but didn't ask me up to her rooms, as she sometimes did.

I don't think I minded very much.

THAT CONVERSATION WITH KIRK at The Stag took place, as I say, just a few days after I saw him outside the Pharmacy window. So when the defacing (apt word) of the Monument occurred, I made a point of going over to the Keep and telling Sentinel Hogg he ought to keep watch on our visitor, the Colonial. I said I had an uncomfortable feeling about him.

The Sentinel advised me to leave the worrying to him.

As for the Monument, the attempts made to repair it have transformed it. The plaster that fills the hollows of the ruined faces has given them a menacing, zombie look. But that effect is quite negated by the plaster triangle in the area of the woman's groin: Liberty looks as though she's wearing underpants now.

It was during the time when the repairs were being done that I told Anna the dream I'd had about the collie and how I'd beaten it and how it wouldn't die. Anna and I were sitting in the cafe at the time.

"Perhaps something needs to get out of you, and you're trying to stop it," she said. "Or perhaps you're trying to drive something out and it won't leave."

Her comments on my dreams (whenever I chose to reveal them to her) were always astute. She never remembers her own dreams, or so she says. But she seems so intimate with their strangeness I don't know if I quite believe her.

Sitting there in the cafe quietly drinking coffee, I raised the matter that was most on my mind.

"I hear you and Kirk have become very friendly over the last week."

She was quite composed.

"Yes, we have."

I didn't ask her if it was true she'd taken Kirk up to her rooms, or that she'd already spent a night in his room in The Stag. Mitchell had reported these things to me.

"Anna, I rely on you. We all do."

"I know you do."

And we left it at that.

SEVEN DAYS PASSED AFTER the vandalism at the Monument, and nothing else extraordinary happened in Carrick. I was busy with Pharmacy matters, but often early in the morning, I'd catch a glimpse of the Colonial with his fishing-rod and his box, passing behind the Monument and the cluster of pines on his way up to the hills. The days were mainly cold, or overcast, or wet, or foggy, or all of these. I wondered what effect the weather was having on Kirk.

On the morning of the eighth day, a Sunday, any complacency Carrick might have begun to feel was disrupted.

I'd had another disturbed night, and was awakened before dawn by a hammering noise: it was the knocking of an airlock in the cold water pipe that ran through the wall behind my bed. I lay for a while trying to squirm my way back into the entrance of a dream I couldn't quite remember. But the exertion of squeezing myself into that ever-narrowing opening only made me more awake.

I rose and brewed some coffee to counter the chill in my bones. I'd hardly begun to drink it when I heard another hammering, this time from downstairs. Someone was rapping at the window. I took a deep breath and went down into the darkened store. Outside, I could see figures in oilskins carrying flashlights, Sentinel Hogg among them.

I opened the door. It was raining and the morning was still dark. The street was oily in the fog.

"Robert. I'm glad you're awake," said the Sentinel. "Would you come with us? Something's wrong down at the graveyard."

I looked around them all, a dozen men in oilskins and sou'westers, anonymous as monks, but familiar from their shapes — Hawthorn, Kennedy, Cameron and Thomson among them.

"I'll be ready in a minute."

DURING THE WALK TO THE GRAVEYARD a mile west of Carrick on the coast road, Sentinel Hogg told me what was wrong:

"Cameron was driving back from Lannock in the fog with the morning bread. He almost hit a rock lying in the middle of the road. He got out to move it, but it wasn't a rock."

There was no other talking, only the crunch of boots on the roadway. The noise was louder as we passed the place where the road intersects the remains of the old wall Kirk had asked about that night in The Stag. It's really only a rampart of earth covered in rocks like a huge set of gums and broken teeth. The people here built it more than a thousand years ago and it girdles the countryside for mile after mile. The live bodies of virgins were supposed to be interred in it to make it last. Whether the purpose of the wall was to keep something in or out, no one can say any more.

Beyond the wall, we passed an area of marshland with a centuries-old stink. As children, we used to make believe the smell was caused by ooze from the graveyard seeping into the marsh. We enjoyed the way it dragged at our feet, causing us to walk with the jerky steps of puppets. We pretended some demon of the marsh was trying to pull us down.

After the marsh, the beams from our flashlights lit up the road by the graveyard. We saw the debris Cameron had seen. Not rocks, but a gravestone, broken to pieces; and, further along, a statue, armless and headless.

We went over to the graveyard itself. It's centuries old, too, and surrounded by a chest-high stone wall; on top, an ornate iron chain links together a series of gargoyles. Our group, moving cautiously now, couldn't see far in, just some headstones that seemed to peg down the edges of the fog. On the margin of our lights, darker outlines were lurking. They might have been creatures bent over the graves but we were aware they were only bushes.

The iron gate was ajar. Sentinel Hogg pushed against the dripping cross bars to open it wider, wiped his hands on his coat, and went inside.

We followed him in and along the central walkway between the plots. Our flashlights illuminated the steaming mounds of graves and the ranks of headstones ("exit-markers," my father, Alexander Aiken, called them; "some people spend their lives searching for their own," he'd say). Many of them were made of concrete, and would deteriorate at a pace not much slower than the bodies they commemorated; others were of marble, and testified to the durability of stone over flesh.

As we advanced deeper into the graveyard, nothing seemed unusual except for our presence there at this time of day.

Then Sentinel Hogg, who was a little in front of me, stumbled against something. His flashlight lit up the disembodied head of a woman with bright red lips. He prodded it with his boot and we saw no blood, no veins severed at the neck. It was a statue's head, but the mouth had been smeared with lipstick.

That was the beginning of the devastation. From there on, the pathway we walked along was strewn with shattered headstones, shards of burial urns, broken crosses and angels' wings. The workmanship of generations of masons and sculptors lay in ruins.

In the middle of the graveyard we came upon a number of broken and uprooted memorial tablets arranged in a ring. In the centre, one stone angel was lying on top of another, each with its face in the other's groin. On the uppermost angel's back, a circle the size of a soup-plate had been sprayed thickly with bright red paint.

"I've seen enough," Sentinel Hogg said. "We'll come back at daylight."

So we began to retreat in a group, careful to avoid tripping over the debris. Near the gate, along one of the side paths, we saw what looked like a freshly dug grave.

"Let's take a quick look," the Sentinel said.

We were reluctant but went with him to the grave and shone our flashlights into the hole. It had been partly refilled with earth. The long-handled sexton's shovel was lying on a heap of clay nearby and Sentinel Hogg picked it up. He leaned over and prodded for a few seconds at the fresh earth in the grave.

We were all looking down, and saw for ourselves what happened. In fact, we should have been able to predict it, we should have been able to laugh at it — it was the kind of thing only children believe might happen on such a night, in such a place. As we watched, the earth began to stir of its own accord as though something down there were moving under it, pushing up. All at once, the clay erupted, and out burst a hairy arm with a cloven hand, trembling with power, reaching up towards us.

I don't know who it was that lost his nerve first, but someone started running, and the others followed. Only Sentinel Hogg and Cameron and I didn't run, though we walked quickly enough after the others, out through the gate and back up the road towards Carrick. I would have walked faster, and I could see Cameron was just as apprehensive, but Sentinel Hogg restrained us, defying our fears.

When we reached Carrick, the men who'd run stood waiting for us outside the Keep. The Green was foggy and the other buildings were barely visible except for the Church and the Library; they loomed like massive weights holding down the ephemeral world. Sentinel Hogg unlocked the door of the Keep and together, those who had run and those who hadn't, we went inside and waited for the light.

ALL THROUGH THAT DAY and for most of that week, the townspeople scoured the graveyard for fragments, even the most minuscule, to restore the tablets and the statuary. It was like assembling some vast jigsaw puzzle. Many of the gravestones when they were restored had the look of cracked eggshells; others were half-patched together like scarred buildings among the rubble of a bombed city.

The townspeople made special attempts to piece together the inscriptions, for it was the custom in Carrick when a family member died to rub some of the blood of surviving relatives into the grooves of the sculpted name. My own father's stone was broken in so many pieces it wasn't worthwhile trying to restore it. The marker over the grave of Anna's parents had not been so badly smashed, and I offered her my help. She thanked me but said Kirk had already volunteered.

No one, so far as I could tell, made any effort to tamper with that ring of stones in the middle of the graveyard. The two angels continued to lie on top of each other, head to groin, as though they were part of some erotic mythology.

As for the cloven hand that reached up to us from the grave that dark morning, we saw by daylight that it was only the hoof of a dead sheep, still protruding stiffly. How it got there, we all wondered. Campbell, the sexton, said so far as he was concerned no human being would ever be buried in that grave; he just left the sheep in it and shovelled in the rest of the dirt.

I made a point of visiting Sentinel Hogg at the Keep. I told him again about my suspicion of Kirk. I pointed out to him that not all of the gravestones had been vandalized equally; that in some cases, such as my father Alexander's, the damage was savage. I said, too, that I hoped he'd taken particular note of the circle painted on the angel's back.

He shuffled his big body, and his short neck reddened.

"I saw everything you saw, Robert. Now, please. Let me do things my own way." His wooden chair creaked noisily.

"Shouldn't we at least have a meeting of the Council?" I asked.

His eyes, as they often did, began to strobe around as though he were afraid they might obliterate me, or anything else they rested on too long.

"I'll think about it."

ON ANOTHER EVENING THAT WEEK just before closing time, Miss Balfour, who happens to be a Council member, came into the Pharmacy. She is very elderly, with skin like parchment. She wanted some bee-sting elixir; she'd been stung (as had so many townspeople) by one of these out-of-season bees. It was unusual to see her in the Pharmacy, though she'd been a frequent visitor when my father, Alexander, was alive. She helped look after me when I was a child.

"Might I have the benefit of your thoughts on this matter, Robert?" she asked, enunciating her words with great precision. She wears high-necked sweaters, to cover a mole in the middle of her neck; it often peeps out spitefully as she talks and it did now. "Please enlighten me."

"Thoughts on what?" I asked.

"These dreadful mutilations." She relished the word. "Who among us would perpetrate such atrocities? Our own townspeople would never defile their past."

"Perhaps the Council should meet," I said. "Perhaps

we ought to talk about what's going on." I gave her the package of medication, and as she counted out the price under the counter lamp, I noted how visible were her finger bones beneath the flesh.

"I agree with you, Robert," she said. "I shall speak to the Sentinel. I greatly fear matters are going to worsen."

Through the window, I watched her go out onto the Green. She disintegrated for a while in the dark, till a rope of light from the street lamp on the far side pulled her into existence again.

SHORTLY AFTER SHE LEFT, I locked up (we'd all begun locking doors and windows now in Carrick) and went to The Stag for dinner. There was no sign of Kirk in the dining-room or in the bar, so I ate alone and around eight I headed back to the Pharmacy. The night had turned bitingly cold and the town was quiet, waiting perhaps for something to happen. As I passed Anna's store, I noticed the lights on in her rooms above. I thought of knocking, as I once would have; now I hesitated and decided against it.

Back at the Pharmacy I saw a piece of paper had been slipped under the door. I held it over towards the light coming through the window and read the heavy hand-writing:

Robert:

Meeting of the Council, re. the Colonial.
4 tomorrow at Dr R's.

Hogg

THE NEXT AFTERNOON WHEN I left the store to go to the Council meeting, the sky was a dark boulder on the edge of the eastern hills. As I walked to Doctor Rankin's, my fingers automatically strummed the skeletal privet hedge that borders the laneway. The house is a squat two-storey granite building with a front yard protected from the lane by a railing of iron spikes. The red-painted steps below the ivied doorway give the impression of lipstick on a whiskered mouth.

The little nun of a woman in maid's uniform who answered the bell has been Doctor Rankin's maid all my life. She led me to the study; its walls are lined with mahogany bookcases full of heavy medical books that absorb most of whatever light filters through the narrow window at the north end.

Round the oblong table my fellow councillors sat. Sentinel Hogg was fussing with some papers. Miss Balfour's head was turned towards the window, but the mole on her neck was focused on me.

I took my place just as Doctor Rankin appeared. He's a small, thin man in his seventies with heavy footsteps, like a man who was once fat (he never was) and his body hadn't yet learnt to adjust to lightness. He sat down in his high-backed chair and nodded to Sentinel Hogg to begin the meeting.

The Sentinel cleared his throat. Words make him uncomfortable — as though they're too small for his big body to control. When he speaks you can't help thinking of some otherwise placid field animal swatting away flies with its tail.

"Robert and Miss Balfour are worried about the

Colonial, Kirk," he said, looking around the table. No hummingbird's wings flitted more rapidly than the Sentinel's eyelashes. Then he looked down at his papers again; his introduction of the topic, purely for the benefit of Doctor Rankin, was over. It was up to me now.

"The two incidents took place not long after Kirk's arrival," I said. "He's too curious about Carrick. The fact is, I don't trust him."

"He's a frequent visitor to the Library," said Miss Balfour. "From the very first time he appeared, he's shown considerable interest in our history." As ever, when she spoke, she mouthed the words so meticulously they might have been razor blades. "He was particularly curious about the situation here during the War. Of course I felt obliged to familiarize him with the location of the appropriate books. Did I act improperly?" Her mole bobbed up and down, playing peekaboo.

Sentinel Hogg spoke again with a great effort.

"Mitchell's keeping an eye on him. He says Kirk spends a lot of time in his room when he's not in the hills." His eyes flickered in my direction. "Up in his room, often. Kirk and Anna."

I kept silent though I could feel the two names quivering in my brain like javelins. I waited for Doctor Rankin's opinion. He usually had the last word in our decisions. He cleared his throat and spoke at last in barely more than a whisper.

"The Colonial came to see me just yesterday. He showed me maps of water levels and reservoirs. He wanted to know where we get our drinking water. He asked a host of questions about the St Giles Pond."

He gestured with the thin fingers of his right hand; for a moment, his nails seemed to surprise him, and he studied them. "He was especially curious about the closing of the Mine." He rubbed his nose with his finger.

As a child lying on my back on his examination table, I used to clutch the table for fear of levitating into those inverted venus flytraps, his nostrils. I used to believe it wouldn't be possible to deceive someone who knew the mysteries of the flesh as intimately as he did.

"I told him no more than I would tell anyone who asks," he said, "but he wasn't satisfied. We must all be very careful indeed."

"Very well," the Sentinel nodded. "I've sent to Security Headquarters for information on him. They don't like mystery men any more than we do. We should also try to find out what he's doing in the hills. Agreed?"

We did agree and the meeting was quickly over, as our meetings usually were. I always found them interesting, so much said in so few words. We filed outside and hunched into the dark and the cold drizzle, a harbinger perhaps of snow. At the Green, we parted for our various destinations: Miss Balfour, to open the Library for the evening; Sentinel Hogg to the Keep and his eternal paper work; and I to the Pharmacy to mix compounds for bee elixirs. Then, a can of soup (I wasn't in the mood for The Stag), a book, my meditations and bed.

THE MORNING AFTER THAT meeting was the first of February. Mitchell called at the Keep early and told Sentinel Hogg that Kirk had asked for sandwiches for his lunch; that meant he was going up into the hills for the entire day. The Sentinel in turn came to see me. He suggested this might be a good opportunity for me to follow Kirk and watch his activities. I said I would.

That was one of those rare winter mornings, bright and only a little cold. The sun shone and the townspeople who were up early pretended to know how to behave in sunshine, smiling to each other in the street around the Green. An outsider might have been fooled by the change in the weather and have hoped for even better things. But we knew that the puffs of fog that lay in the high furrows of the hills would swell like dough and spill over into the valley by nightfall.

I stood at the store window in my rubber boots, sipping my coffee, watching. Around nine o'clock, I saw Kirk come out of The Stag into the sunshine. He was wearing his green hiking sweater and his boots, and he had his black tin box slung over his shoulder. But he wasn't playing the sportsman any longer: he carried no fishing-rod.

He began walking eastward at a brisk pace so I slid my binoculars into my coat pocket, put the CLOSED sign in the window and set out after Kirk. The villagers who were enjoying the sun called out encouragement to me. As I passed Anna's store, I saw her at the window; but the glass was brilliant in the sun and I couldn't make out the expression on her face.

The road climbs gradually for a half-mile east of the village till it forks. After that, it becomes not much more than a gravel track. The southern branch swings round the hillsides past several cottages; the other branch, which leads to the Mine, is overgrown now. That was the one Kirk took; it leads north-east, behind the Cairn, which is the nearest of the hills called the Knuckles (an old ballad says a demon is buried near Carrick and these hills are the knuckles of his left hand). I stayed well back, about a quarter-mile behind Kirk, following him even when he left the road and started across country. Up here on such a day, I had no trouble seeing him; in fact, I had to be careful for he might as easily see me.

Soon we were well up into the rough apron of moors around the bases of the hills. Every time Kirk reached a stream, he'd stop for a few minutes. Once, he disturbed some moor-birds and as they wheeled and yelped, he looked back. I dropped to the bracken, burying my nose in its earthy smell. When I looked up again he was on the move. I wondered whether he knew he was being followed, perhaps even knew who was following him, and had decided to play his part so long as I played mine.

I was sure by now that he was headed for the area of the St Giles Pond and the old Mine, and that he was going the long way — parallel to the road, and behind the Cairn. I decided to cut directly north by the shorter, more dangerous way across the marshes.

This was where my father, Alexander, used to come to collect plants. In these marshes grow the long-rooted gorse, from which he'd make diuretics and anaesthetics; here are clumps of the rare black heather he used for his cough mixtures — their aroma is so enduring I could smell it on that February day; the dwarf bracken grows here, too — an emetic that can be deadly if it isn't prepared properly.

"A cure can be a poison," my father often told me when I was learning the trade, "and a poison can be a cure. Amusing, isn't it?" He never laughed when he said this.

After wading through the marshes for a quarter of an hour, I reached dry land and the Monolith. It's a rock twenty feet tall, abandoned there in some ancient shift of the earth. Niches worn by time and weather have been gouged out of its southern belly. I began climbing up very carefully, for a thick layer of moss coats the niches. When I slithered over into the hollow at the top, my boot punctured a little eye of water that stared upward.

I settled myself as comfortably as I could and focused the binoculars on the moors north of the Cairn. I could see the St Giles Pond shimmering in the distance, and further along, the scar of the road and the old Mine. After a while, Kirk himself appeared round the hip of the Cairn.

It's a curiously intimate experience to watch someone through binoculars. As he walked, I could see Kirk's lips move, and he'd smile as though he were telling himself something amusing or wise. After one of these silent utterances, he stooped beside a stream, and I had a clear view of him practising his trade. He opened his black box, took out a glass tube and scooped up some water with it. From a bottle, he measured out some powder into the tube, shook the mixture then held it up to the sky and examined it. After that, he spilled the water back into the stream and rinsed the tube. He took out a notebook and wrote in it briefly. I could see so clearly that if he'd held the book at the right angle, I might even have been able to read what he was writing.

He closed the box, straightened up, then slowly turned and stared in the direction of the Monolith, his eyes looking right into mine. I ducked below the rim. I lay there, thinking: surely he can't have seen me from that distance? and wondering: how much can he see?

I stayed out of sight. When I looked over the rim again, Kirk's back was to me and he'd reached a flat area not far from the St Giles Pond and the Mine. He was walking around it slowly, looking down into the bracken.

That, too, was a place I knew well. When I was a boy, along with others I searched in the same stretch of bracken. The only one of us who ever came across anything was Cameron, when he was about twelve. He found a coin with a strange inscription on it and brought it home. His father took it from him and told all of us to forget it ever existed.

A whistle split the silence. The air currents brought it to me first, higher up as I was. Kirk heard it an instant later and looked towards the north. Then he waved. I swung the glasses round past the dormant bracken and heather, past a scattering of grey sheep, past the black-and-white flare of two collies. Then I settled on the whistler himself in his dark skip cap, his neck bundled up with a plaid scarf.

My heart sank into the cold rock. The whistler was Adam Swainston.

I watched him and Kirk move across the moor towards each other like flies traversing a huge expanse of table. Through the binoculars I saw them meet and shake hands, then sit among the bracken. Swainston pulled out his pipe and lit up; Kirk unpacked his sandwiches and began eating. One thing was clear: these two men were no strangers to each other.

I'd seen what I came to see. I climbed down carefully from the rock and made my way through the marshes back to Carrick. In the town, several of the townspeople were still standing around the Green. They looked at me inquisitively, but I spoke to no one and and went straight to the Keep. The same townspeople were still watching as Sentinel Hogg and I came out of the Keep together and visited Anna in her store. And still they were watching when we left her. By then, the noon hour had passed, and everything was arranged.

THAT NIGHT AT THE STAG around nine-thirty, Mitchell brought me to the guest room next to Kirk's. He pushed the wardrobe to one side and showed me a trim hole in the wall at eye-height. The carpet under the hole was well worn.

"It's all yours for tonight," he said, leaving me.

Through the hole, past a grille and a vase of paper tulips, I could see most of Kirk's room. So I settled down and waited. And waited.

After a long time, I began to think I might be wasting the night. But at about eleven o'clock I heard a voice in the corridor outside and I took up my position. Through the peep-hole, I saw the door of Kirk's room open, and he and Anna came in. He was talking, she was silent. He switched on the light and shut the door behind them, shutting out all the rest of the universe. He took her in his arms and standing there, kissed her.

"Anna, Anna," I heard him say, over and again.

She whispered a reply that wasn't for my ears.

Still standing, Kirk carefully pulled the green sweater up from her waistband and over her head. As he began feeling for the catch on her bra, she said, "Just a moment," and she stretched over and switched off the light.

I was disappointed at that: I'd never given up loving Anna's nakedness.

For a minute, I could hear nothing but rustling and murmuring in the dark room and the creak of bedsprings. Then the filtered light of the street lamps began to block in the shapes of the desk, the chair, the door. And, gradually, their bodies upon the bed. The stuffy heat of the room made it unnecessary for them to cover themselves with the blankets. He was talking to her desperately — words, it seemed to me, of endearment and lust. Then the two figures became one writhing animal, a white beast of many limbs. The writhing became urgent and rhythmic with a frenzy of gasping and Anna's familiar squeals. Then the beast became two again and the two parts lay still; and after a while the two voices reached me as Anna and Kirk began to talk quietly.

As I listened to them, I envied them that intimate exchange of words even more than their love-making. Kirk was doing most of the talking, and was nuzzling into Anna; occasionally I thought I heard the word "love" from him, though not her reply. But, at a certain point, as I knew she must, she sat up and spoke in a clear voice.

"You must tell me this, Kirk. So much depends upon it." She took a deep breath: "Are you the one responsible for the vandalism?"

A long pause followed.

"Why do you ask?" Kirk replied. He sounded weary.

Anna kept to her task.

"What have you been talking to Adam Swainston about?"

She was sitting with her arms on her bent knees, waiting for his answer, the light of the street light softly illuminating her flesh. He did not sit up.

"They've been watching me?"

"What has Swainston been telling you?" She was relentless.

He took a long time before answering, and again it was question for question.

"Anna, do you know what happened long ago here, in Carrick?"

"What does any of it have to do with you?" She was pleading with him. "Why can't you leave it alone? Please leave it alone."

"I can't."

"Then I must leave you alone." Her voice was flat.

"If you must, you must," he said.

It was near midnight when he said that. I watched Anna get out of bed and mime her way along the wall by the door to the light switch. She found it, turned on the light and began to dress, careless of whose eyes might be watching.

Kirk got out of bed too, his wiry body much darker than hers. He wanted to walk her home but she told him she had lived in Carrick town all her life and knew her way without the help of a stranger. In the guise of assisting her with her clothes, he caressed her, running his hands over her as though he were running seeds through his fingers. She brushed them away, finished dressing and left without a word.

In the darkness after she had gone, Kirk stood at the window. He was motionless for many minutes, watching her, I supposed, cross the Green and enter her store. Then slowly, he climbed back into bed.

It was long past midnight when I went downstairs and through the empty lobby and out into the street. The weather had changed to fog mixed with a cold drizzle. The fog on the Green was so thick the far side was quite obliterated. I walked round the long way, the lit way. It was a curious thing how, as I passed under each street light, my shadow would leap away from me and scurry under the lid of the darkness.

ON TUESDAY THE SIXTH of February, at nine-thirty in the morning, I was behind the Pharmacy counter preparing a new batch of my father's special elixir. The phone rang.

"Robert." It was Sentinel Hogg. "Come to the Library. Something's happened."

Through my window I saw Anna already making her way across the Green, so I buttoned my coat and hurried out to walk with her. The morning sun (what there was of it behind the eastern clouds) had been eclipsed by an orange orb. The air was calm. We had to wade through a lagoon of low fog: the Monument was the carved figurehead of a sunken ship; wispy canals separated the buildings on the far shore.

At the entrance to the Library, we made our way

through an anxious group of townspeople. I told them we knew no more than they did. We climbed the six worn granite steps to the heavy wooden door. I held it open for Anna and we went in, and up the echoing staircase to the landing, then through the glass door into the Library itself.

Inside, everything seemed neat as ever. But in spite of my warm coat the building was bitterly cold, and the smell of floor polish was more austere than ever. Our breath trumpeted out as though we were in an alien element. From the far corner of the reading area, behind the last rows of bookshelves, we could hear voices and the clatter of shoes on the wooden floor. We went in that direction.

Sentinel Hogg was there, holding a handkerchief to his nose; he was examining something extraordinary: a miniature waterfall in a place where no waterfall could be. Yet, there it was — white foam slowly pouring down from a height, a mist rising at the base. This waterfall which could not be a waterfall covered all the front of one of the bookcases. Above it, still visible, was the sign: CARRICK — BOOKS AND JOURNALS.

"Acid!" Miss Balfour said this. She was standing near the bookcase and had seen us coming. "The Sentinel's under the impression it's some kind of acid." Her mole had shrunk out of sight, and the nose in her parchment face was blue. Her voice echoed through the Library as she elaborated. "He believes someone has poured acid over our books."

Something bitter, but with no smell, irritated my nose. Through the foam I could make out the pitted spines of the books, the corroding titles. The acid had already begun its warping effect even on the wooden shelves so that they looked as though they might, in due course, take on the shapes of trees again.

"If it's libracetic acid," I said to the Sentinel, "you'd better not touch anything. It's very strong."

"Look at that," Miss Balfour said. She pointed to the far end of the shelves, to the blackboard used for Library announcements. On it a crude sketch had been drawn of a female form with highlighted breasts and crotch. In the middle of its enlongated neck was an emphatic spot, like a third nipple.

Sentinel Hogg was wiping his nose with his handkerchief. His face was pinched with the cold and the acid.

"Come and see this," he said, and showed us where, on the end of the bookcase, a red circle had been sprayed. Then he asked me: "Can we do anything about the books?"

"It takes at least twenty-four hours for this acid to neutralize," I said. "The books are ruined."

THERE WAS NOTHING MORE to do. All four of us stood for a while, watching the foam softly eating the books away. Then we left. Anna had not said a word.

A bigger group of townspeople was gathered at the steps now. Hawthorn was among them, and Kennedy with his wife; the Thomsons were there, as well as Hewson and Cameron. Sentinel Hogg told them briefly about the destruction of the books. They listened quietly in the calm morning. The Sentinel said if any of them had seen anything or heard anything that might help, he'd be in the Keep all day, and they should come and talk to him. I noticed how Anna glanced up once or twice at Kirk's window in The Stag; but I saw no sign of movement from there.

Then the Sentinel and Anna and I walked across the Green. When we reached her store, she did not invite us upstairs for coffee as she normally would. The Sentinel spoke to her softly:

"And you, Anna? Do you have something you want to tell me?"

With a closed face, she looked at him, then at me.

"I've kept away from Kirk. I haven't slept with him and I haven't talked to him since that night you were listening."

She went inside without another word.

The Sentinel and I walked on to the Pharmacy.

"I just wanted to give her a chance to speak out," he said. "It's not always easy."

"Sentinel," I said. "When do you intend to put a stop to all this?"

"In due course," he said, "in due course. I'm waiting for word from Security Headquarters." His face was pale in the cold air. "I hope things don't get out of hand." He nodded goodbye and walked away towards the Keep.

THAT NIGHT IN THE BAR of The Stag, Kirk was sitting at one of the wall tables when I arrived. Everything was very quiet; I couldn't hear the taped music or the sounds of doors shutting in other parts of the building.

"Silent as the grave," said Mitchell, serving me.

Kirk had seen me and signalled me to come and sit beside him. Carrick was on his mind — Carrick in the old days. He wanted to ask me questions and I made no attempt to stop him.

"What happened to the old church next door?" he asked. "Is it never used?"

"It's been closed for a long time — since the end of the War, at least. Alexander Aiken, my father, said we don't need churches any more. He said we've learnt everything the Great Executioner in the Sky had to teach."

"Your father must have been very cynical." He did not smile, but kept pecking out questions in a predatory way: "What about the Festival? Why was it abandoned?"

"You'd have to ask one of the old people," I said. "It was their decision."

"Which one of them could I trust to tell me the truth?" he asked.

I assumed he didn't really expect an answer to that, so I asked him a question.

"You know what happened at the Library this morning?"

"Know?" He was alert. "I don't *know* anything. Some books were ruined, weren't they? I heard acid was used."

"These acts of vandalism," I said, "do you think they're all connected?"

"If you mean do I think the same person is behind them all, yes. Why not? Perhaps someone wants to wipe out the history of Carrick." He then used words that were more or less the same as those of Miss Balfour. "I don't think you've seen the end of it."

"What do you mean?"

"Now why would I mean something?" His eyes were blue and clear and cold. "I don't mean anything. I don't mean a single thing. Not one single thing."

SENTINEL HOGG TOLD ME on the Wednesday afternoon that he was going up to Swainston's cottage to have a chat about Kirk. He set out in the black police car. The sun had been shining all morning, and many of the townspeople were again out on the Green pretending they preferred this kind of weather, that they could see just as clearly in sunshine as in more discreet light.

I went to my upstairs window and watched for the Sentinel with my binoculars (once, years ago, when I was at my window looking round the Green with my binoculars, I settled on Kennedy's rooms, and found that he was watching *me* through *his* binoculars. I must admit, I was surprised that he should think it worthwhile watching me). The police car was out of sight at first then came into view when it reached the gravel road that runs south of Carrick to some cottages, then on into the high moors. Even up there I could see the same pretence going on as here in the town: when the car passed a small ash tree, a leaf pirouetted to the ground as though this were only October and not the dead of winter.

After a mile, the car came to a halt by the approach path to Swainston's cottage. I watched the Sentinel's every move.

He left the car and walked along the path through the winter heather. He crossed the small humped bridge built by would-be invaders almost two thousand years ago. He was breathing heavily as he climbed the path to the cottage, a cube of a building. He stood for a moment examining the eastern gable that was invisible to me. He turned and looked back towards Carrick; he'd be able to see, on a day like this, all of the buildings around the Green and the minute townspeople going about their business. He knew I'd be watching him.

He walked then to Swainston's door and knocked. Two collies appeared from the back of the cottage with their tails wagging. He patted them, and waited, and knocked again. He tried the door handle. The door swung open and he went in; the collies waited outside.

I could only imagine what he might see in there: the sunlight streaming into the living-room through the mullioned windows onto sheepskin rugs; the clean, rough kitchen; Swainston, perhaps, at his lunch.

But no, I knew he couldn't have seen Swainston, for he emerged from the front door again after only a few seconds. He closed it behind him and stood for a while. Then, with the collies leading him, he walked slowly round past the western gable to the back of the cottage and out of my sight again. The only other movement I noticed was from several sheep grazing higher up the slopes.

When the Sentinel reappeared, he was half-running. He lumbered along the path from the cottage back to his car. He climbed in, reversed, then sped back along the road that would eventually join the paved road down to Carrick.

I'D ALERTED KENNEDY and Hawthorn, both of them members of the Carrick Volunteer Fire Brigade, by the time Sentinel Hogg returned to the town. We greeted him and agreed to accompany him back up to the cottage. He told us it wouldn't be pleasant, but we were prepared for that. My father, Alexander Aiken, often said that those who live their lives surrounded by nature have been schooled in unpleasantness by the finest teacher.

Kennedy drove the fire brigade van, and the rest of us, Hawthorn, Sentinel Hogg and I sat in the back. We didn't talk, both because of the noise of the van's wheels on gravel and because we were apprehensive. Kennedy parked with a jolt at the narrow bridge.

Even from there, fifty yards from the cottage, we could see what had made the Sentinel pause earlier: a red circle, three feet in diameter, was daubed on the eastern gable.

We carried the stretcher over the bridge and up the path. As we passed the front of the cottage, I squinted through the old-fashioned window with its little thick panes; I could see nothing but a writhing vase of withered flowers on the inside sill and a distorted, neat living-room.

The Sentinel led us over the rough lawn to the back of the cottage where some sheep were grazing. There, on the ground with his back against the stone wall of the sheep pen, his chin on his chest, sat Adam Swainston. His two collies were keeping watch, wagging their tails. Swainston looked for all the world like a man napping, resting his back against the wall; like a man humming in his sleep; like a man with a thick rope of beard from his nose to his navel.

But we knew he wasn't asleep or humming or bearded. He was dead, and the beard was a stalactite of congealed blood covered with thousands of blow flies at a time of the year when there should have been no blow flies. The humming was their thanksgiving hymn as they gorged themselves on a winter feast.

Sentinel Hogg drew Swainston's outline in yellow chalk and organized us around the body, each of us to a limb for lifting. The dogs looked on anxiously but didn't interfere. We lifted in unison and the flies rose too, for they were quite willing to co-operate. But as we laid Swainston on the stretcher, something rolled out of the massed flies and touched Kennedy's foot. He leaped back so fearfully we almost dropped the body.

Whatever it was that had scared Kennedy lay on the grass, the dogs sniffing at it, the flies reassembling on it.

The Sentinel swatted dogs and flies away. The thing on the grass seemed to be a bracelet — some kind of black coral. He bent over it.

"Lips," he said. "His lips have been sliced off." Taking out his handkerchief, he carefully picked up the ring of flesh and laid it on top of the body. I tried not to look at Swainston's face where the lips should have been.

And so we carried all of the shepherd's remains down to the waiting van. I remembered as we walked that the date was Wednesday, the fourteenth of February, the Love Day.

EVERYTHING CAME RAPIDLY to a head now. Sentinel Hogg ordered Kirk confined to his room at The Stag and called in police agents from the Capital. Two beefy men arrived the next morning. They politely asked questions around the town and made notes. I expected them to visit Anna and me, but they didn't. They and the Sentinel spent much of the afternoon with Kirk, then they returned to the Capital that same evening.

For the remainder of the week Kirk went on with his daily expeditions into the hills. Then, on Sunday, a bitterly cold day on which snow again seemed certain, Sentinel Hogg told me he'd received a message: Kirk was to take the Monday morning train to the Capital and present himself at Security Headquarters for interrogation.

I HAD THE BRIEFEST of conversations with Kirk in the bar that Sunday night. When I came in he was sitting near the fire with a Scotch in front of him, resting his head in his arms. I thought he was dozing, but he looked up.

"Tired?" I asked.

The blue ice of his eyes seemed to have thawed. "If only we could cradle our minds as easily," he said.

That was one of the few times I ever saw what might have been a sign of weakness in him.

"You're going to the Capital tomorrow?" I asked.

His eyes were hard again. "Good news travels fast," he said. "Don't worry. I'll be back again in the evening." He swallowed down his Scotch and rose. "You can be certain of one thing. Your troubles aren't over yet," he said. And left.

AT FIVE-THIRTY THE MORNING was black and the fog was thick enough. On such a morning, people up here in the hills live by a kind of faith: though they might be anywhere, they trust that they are where they are. Standing by the Monument, I had to strain my eyes to see Mitchell open the hotel door and Kirk come out into the street. He set out for the railway station. I waited a few seconds, then began to follow him. Mitchell, who was still standing at the door, nodded to me.

That walk along the half-mile lane to the station was a cold one and silent. I walked softly for fear Kirk might hear my very thoughts.

After ten minutes of careful walking I saw the faint aureole of lights from the station, then the shape of Kirk entering the glow, lifting the latch of the gate and going inside. I kept well back and watched him arrange his ticket at the ticket office. Then he sat on a damp bench. The platform was empty but for him at one end, sitting on the bench, and me standing now at the other. In the dim station lights, the rails in their bed of gravel had the look of a well-oiled weapon.

His bench faced south across the tracks to a low privet hedge and the moors sweeping away to the hills. Not that he could see the hills. He just sat staring into the dense fog. I snuggled into my coat against the chill.

The train's vibration reached the station a full minute before any sound. Then the rumble began and drew nearer and nearer, then came the hissing, then the squeal of metal on metal. I stepped forward to the edge of the platform in time to see the black mass of the engine bludgeon the fog apart.

In those seconds, Kirk too must have risen from the bench and he must have walked to the edge of the platform to stand beside me. He must have been there in time to see the steam of the train, whiter than the fog, and the red glow of the furnace.

Then I saw his body sprawled across the tracks, his face towards me.

He may have shouted; he had time to shout. But I heard nothing — not that the engine would have paid any more attention to words than to solid flesh. Kirk lay there, then he was erased by a wall of metal and sparks and flashing lights and clamour.

I didn't wait to find out what he had become. I turned and made my way out of the station away from the noise and hurried back along the lane, staring straight ahead, welcoming the silence and the fog into my mind that morning, Kirk's last morning in Carrick, and in this world.

THE SAME TWO BEEFY police agents returned again to Carrick. Again they were polite, and so were we. Again they asked more questions around the town, and again they didn't speak to me or to Anna. They spent most of the time with Sentinel Hogg. He helped them arrive at an uncomplicated conclusion that ensured they wouldn't have to prolong their stay in Carrick. Kirk must have killed Swainston, they decided; then he himself had committed suicide by jumping in front of the train. Now what could be simpler than that? It was a straightforward case of guilt in pursuit of punishment.

Their decision made, they went back to the Capital.

SOME OF THE TOWNSPEOPLE may have regret-ted the loss of Swainston, but only Anna seemed to mourn Kirk's death. For the most part, Carrick was ready to swing into its old ways.

"Life must go on." So the townspeople said.

The first time I heard that was from the wife of the shepherd Bromley. He was a small man; she was a woman with a neat, feline face that was at odds with her shapeless lump of a body. She'd come to the Pharmacy for some of my father's elixir for Bromley who'd been stung on the neck by one of the out-of-season bees. That day in the Pharmacy, she said complacently: "Bromley says life must go on."

I thought it unwise of her and the others to discard their caution so quickly. But I said: "Perhaps. Perhaps."

ACCORDINGLY THE FIRST reports about the rabbits didn't cause much concern to the people of Carrick. The rabbits, hundreds of them, began dying in the moors up by the Cairn. So many died that even though hawks, water-rats, weasels and other connoisseurs of putrid rabbit meat congregated from miles around, they could devour only a fraction of the available supply. Shepherds and fishermen complained about stumbling over the corpses of rabbits that rotted away in every valley and hillside. The first person to actually witness one of the rabbit deaths was Vernon, a lanky shepherd who kept a flock on the west side of the Cairn.

I met him in the cafe just the morning after the two agents left Carrick. He told me that on his way down to the village, a big moorland rabbit had come running straight at him. He'd seen it darting along the hill above him and knew something was wrong with it. Every few yards it would veer off at an angle as though it were being chased by some predator that was about to strike. Then it headed right at Vernon, on the path, in a most unrabbit-like manoeuvre. He stood still and it came to a halt beside his boots and crouched there. Vernon bent down and fondled its ears and cooed to it. It showed absolutely no fear of his touch. He in his turn realized then that whatever was chasing it was not outside, but within, and that it had this rabbit in a death grip. The rabbit lay on its side with its head resting on Vernon's right boot. In less than a minute, its quick rabbit breathing stopped, its eyes clouded over and it was dead.

"Have you seen anything like that before?" I asked Vernon this because he was a man who'd herded sheep and snared rabbits in the hills for forty years. He wiped his long nose with his sleeve.

"No. I don't believe I ever have," he said.

BUT CARRICK WASN'T WORRIED at that point, as I said. At least not very much. So what if rabbits were dying up in the hills, even in quantities? They were a nuisance — good riddance to them.

Then there was the matter of the fish. Some townspeople who fished the St Giles Pond said a lot of the fish were acting strangely. When they were hooked, they didn't fight; they just swam around in the pond in tighter and tighter circles before rising to the surface, belly up. Or when they were landed, they didn't thrash about, but lay in the bracken, quite placid.

The fishermen got no pleasure out of catching fish that didn't mind being caught. But they blamed the excess of rain for the problem. These winter spates in the streams that fed the pond always disoriented the fish, they said. Granted the numbers of crazy fish were very large this year, granted a lot of fish were dying even without the assistance of the fishermen — but their deaths were from natural causes.

Even when the shepherd Cummings's two collies sickened and died, none of the townspeople was that alarmed. Everyone was sorry about the dogs, but dogs will be dogs, won't they? No doubt they'd eaten some of the putrescent rabbits and the fish that were strewn on the banks of every stream in the moors around the Cairn.

The day after his dogs died, I saw Cummings crossing the Green and I went out to talk to him. He was a taciturn man who hid behind a grey beard and who always had a limp of some sort. I expected it would take a long time to coax the story out of him, so I was surprised when he recited it to me as though it were a prepared speech.

"About six in the morning," he said, "I went to the door and whistled to the two dogs the way I always do to come for some food before we took the sheep up into the high moors. I knew those dogs were sick right away. They came crawling on their bellies from the side of the house where their hutch is. They were dragging their hind legs and they were afraid I'd be mad at them for being sick. I lifted them into the house and they lay on the floor, staring at me, and every time I looked at them they'd wag their tails. About nine in the morning, they started barking. They did that for about five minutes. And then they just died."

For Cummings, this was a very long speech. At the time, I presumed grief over the death of his dogs must have loosened his tongue.

SHORTLY AFTER THAT the sheep began to die; but the people of Carrick still made excuses. Sheep? Don't talk to us about sheep, they said. Sheep are such silly creatures, they said. Always doing one silly thing or another, or dying because of one silly thing or another. Anybody who lives in sheep country, they said, knows sheep are silly.

So the townspeople said, over and over again. But I knew that at last they were beginning to worry and worry.

They had good cause. For now, the first of the human inhabitants of Carrick fell to the illness.

It happened at the one-room Carrick school, a brick building at the top of the lane that runs down to the railway station. Miss Forsyth, the elderly teacher of the town's six school-age children, had been looking out of the staff-room window into the schoolyard, and saw the beginnings of the catastrophe.

Three boys were playing football. Young Cameron, a ten-year-old version of his big-boned father, was running towards the ball when he staggered. Miss Forsyth noted how odd he looked at that instant, the way he lurched backwards as though he'd been shot, and how he stumbled on a few more yards before he collapsed. She saw how he tried to get up again and how his legs betrayed him.

She hurried out into the yard (hurrying was hard for her — she was a heavy woman) to where his friends were looking down at young Cameron with that pitiless curiosity of children. He was smiling up at them. She noted how pale he was, and how the star-shaped birth-mark on the left side of his brow had turned so red it might have been a little red spider on a porcelain vase.

She sent for Doctor Rankin; when he arrived, he ordered the boy to be carried home for observation.

FEBRUARY BLEW ITSELF OUT and passed the baton to energetic March during the week that young Cameron lay in his bed above the bakery. The succulent smells of pies and cakes didn't tempt him to eat though he was a boy who'd rarely been known to refuse food. Nor had he ever been much of a talker. But now he wouldn't keep quiet. He talked and talked, day and night, to himself, to his parents, to anyone who'd listen, exhausting everyone, surprising everyone with the things he said.

One night, for example, he said this to the assembled grown-ups:

"When you take lightly the depths of a child's feelings, you are playing with fire." His parents, and all the other parents there, looked uncomfortable. Later that same night, he spoke directly to his teacher:

"You, Miss Forsyth, must never try to push learning into a child's mind; certain minds only have pull handles." He laughed, but tears rolled down the plump cheeks of Miss Forsyth, a gentle woman.

We were all astonished at young Cameron's insight. He seemed to have been smitten by wisdom as well as by the sickness. But near the end of the week, we noticed that his voice was becoming hoarse and whispery, and his laughter a rasp. One night, after one of those ugly laughs, the little spider on his brow pulsing on and off, on and off, he wanted to say something and we all listened.

"No one understands the depths of crime more profoundly than a child," he whispered loudly. He seemed to be addressing this to me. Anna was with me, and I turned to her to say something, but the look in her eyes made me stop.

ON THE LAST NIGHT around ten o'clock, we couldn't make out what young Cameron was saying any more though that didn't stop him from talking. His parents had to take turns putting their ears to his lips and passing on his words to the rest of us. He'd begun to sweat profusely. At one point, he did become more audible.

"Look at them," we heard him say, gesturing with his arm. "Thousands of them, like a nest of ants on the move." Whatever he was looking at was invisible to us. His eyes were brilliant.

"What are they?" someone asked politely. We'd long ago decided it was best to be polite.

"Words," he said.

At this point, Doctor Rankin, who'd been hovering by the bed on and off for a week, decided it was time to move the boy to the hospital in Stroven, fifty miles north.

Curiously, while we waited for the ambulance to arrive, young Cameron took a turn for the better. He smiled around the room, sat up without help and said he was feeling hungry. At least, we thought that was what he said. But when his mother brought him his favourite meal, beans on toast, he wouldn't touch it.

He just sat there and chattered. We could all hear him now quite plainly, but no one could be sure any more of what he was saying. The sounds coming from his mouth were coherent enough, but either the words were from a language none of us had ever heard (by now, this would not have surprised us), or they were just a kind of demented gibberish.

At two minutes to midnight, he uttered one last burst of sound: "Shackshatl ick apla shatash." He smiled beatifically, then turned onto his side, his spider upward, barely visible. At midnight, the spider disappeared entirely carrying young Cameron's life with it. The ambulance didn't arrive till a half-hour later.

WHEN THE OTHER FIVE children began displaying the symptoms of the illness, Carrick knew for certain that something deadly was in our midst. The children were immediately transported to Stroven Hospital. There, physicians masked themselves against possible contamination and began practising the subtleties of their craft upon the children: they tested (so they informed Doctor Rankin) for Turner's syndrome, Christmas disease, Hartnup's, Milroy's, Niemann-Pick, Woodnig Hoffmann, Huntington's chorea, milzbrand, drysepelas, St Antony's fire, Hansen's disease, Kala azar, dumdum fever, Chagras, Haverhill, frambesia, Kwashiorkor (especially platyhelminth and paragominus), Bantis and Feltes syndromes.

In vain. The illness remained a mystery.

The master healers could only stand by and watch the children, one by one, chatter about this and that till they

61

abruptly died. None of the deaths was in the least painful, just a stopping of the breath.

No adult had so far come down with the illness. These specialists at the Stroven Hospital hypothesized it might only affect children. No sooner had that theory been voiced than the shepherds Vernon, Bromley and Cummings began to display the symptoms. And in rapid order, one adult after another now fell ill.

The decimation of Carrick was under way.

Since there was no known treatment, the specialists decided against bringing all the sick townspeople to Stroven in case the infection spread. Why not allow them to lie in their own beds, and talk, talk, talk and die?

So they remained in their homes in Carrick. Often, wives and husbands lay side by side waiting for death. The Farrances, for example, were bedded together above their shoe store. He was a melancholy man who'd barely spoken to his wife in years; but now he chatted to her endlessly and affectionately, the two of them cooed together like young lovers. On one awkward evening, I, along with other visitors had to leave the bedroom while Farrance attempted to mount his delighted wife. A few days later, they died within minutes of each other.

Others of the townspeople, whose lives had formerly been wretched, actually seemed to blossom under the illness. Campbell, the sexton, for instance. His cadaverous face reflected his profession and the misfortunes that had dogged him all his life: his own mother had died giving birth to him; and when his house burnt down, his wife and daughter had been incinerated in it; he himself had been twitching with palsy for the last twenty years. He succumbed now to the sickness, and his palsy completely vanished as if in compensation. For the first time in years, he could talk about his wife and his daughter without weeping. He looked forward to joining them in the family grave when it came his turn to die.

CARRICK WAS UNDER QUARANTINE now, and traffic was re-routed past it. From my window I saw trucks manned by soldiers in gas masks bringing in supplies. One day, a squad of men erected some Nissen huts at the east end of the town just past the fork that leads towards Swainston's cottage. The huts were to accommodate the soldiers, one or two policemen and the medical team from the Capital. Every day, doctors and nurses in green skull caps and green gowns visited the sick; they analysed, auscultated, experimented, consulted, speculated; they took samples of blood and skin and hair from me and from any other townspeople who were as yet unaffected (the supposition was that in course of time we would all, without exception, be stricken).

The progression from non-human to human deaths made the specialists wonder if some animal disease might be at the root. A group of distinguished veterinarians was invited to Carrick to practise their art: they tested the townspeople for signs of anthrax, charbon, malignant pustule, bighead, blackleg, rinderpest, glanders, aphthous fever, gapes, locoism, pip, staggers, stringhalt, hydrophobia, Texas fever. And anything else they could think of.

But, again, to no avail. The sickness was still a mystery.

I MET REEVE BLAIR, a policeman from Security Headquarters in the Capital. That was yesterday morning when he came to my rooms in the company of two of the medical specialists. He said it was common knowledge that I had a certain mastery of the poisonous properties of local plants. He wondered if I might have any idea what it was that was killing everyone.

As he spoke, I couldn't help thinking of Kirk, with his little black box, bent over the streams; so I asked the two medical men if the Carrick water supply had been carefully checked. They said it had.

"Try again," I said. "You may have been looking for the wrong things." I would tell them nothing more than that.

As they all rose to leave, Reeve Blair said one more thing: "I'll be back to see you soon on other business, Aiken. For now, I've instructed a guard to accompany you when you leave the Pharmacy. For security reasons."

So, in the afternoon when I went on my final climb to the top of the Cairn, I was under guard. When I came back from the climb, Reeve Blair informed me that Anna, and Sentinel Hogg, and Miss Balfour, and Doctor Rankin had fallen sick. I asked the Reeve if I might visit them (I suspected it would be for the last time) and he said yes. My guard came with me and stood outside the doors of their rooms while I had a good discussion with each of them.

We made our decision calmly.

I'M ALONE NOW AT DUSK looking from my upstairs window towards the south side of the Green. The CAFE sign over Kennedy's — the only neon sign in

Carrick — should be illuminated by this time of the day, but it isn't. The light that hissed through its glass veins is still, and not one of the townspeople walks the streets of Carrick any more.

The hulk of the Monument is quite visible, as well as the squat granite shapes of the Church and the Library ("Superstition hand in hand with Knowledge," my father, Alexander, used to say). The whitewashed façade of The Stag stands close to the gloomy Keep further west ("Vice next to Justice," he'd say. "Note that, Robert").

The only other lights in this dusk are the bleared street lamps dangling from their slim gallows.

I can hear the tramp of hobnailed boots. In a minute, the patrol will appear: six soldiers, rifles aslope, marching along the street with their hounds on long leashes. The platoon will stop at intervals, exploring with their flashlights the barred doors and windows. The hounds will sniff here and there casually till some unfamiliar scent stiffens their lean bodies.

The soldiers hate being in Carrick. They hope mainly for one thing: that they'll receive orders to leave. Each day they watch enviously as the ambulances drive away, heading for the northern road to the Capital, screeching in the fog like great crows. Sometimes the hounds join in.

As for me, I sit here alone, looking out on it all. The dim hills in the distance often seem to me now like pages in a great book, with ribbons of fog hanging from them as book marks. I myself may soon be the last word in the book of Carrick.

That was how Aiken's document ended.

The following letter was appended to the last page of it:

Friday, 10:00 A.M.

Maxwell:

Reeve Blair is sitting here in my rooms. He has officially charged me with killing Swainston and Kirk and with poisoning the people of Carrick.

He has read this written account of these last months.

"It's both more than I expected, and less," he says.

"It contains all the ingredients," I say.

"And how am I to know what to do with them?" he says.

"Ah, Reeve," I say. "I practise my craft, and you must practise yours."

I make him a proposition. "Tomorrow, deliver this narrative to your young friend in the Capital" (that's you, Maxwell); "let him come to Carrick, I'll guide him through the mysteries."

The Reeve accepts my offer.

Will you, Maxwell?

We await your decision.

Robert Aiken

What would you have made of it all? For myself, it would be an understatement to say this man Robert Aiken's final message — addressed directly to me — gave me quite a shock. The very fact that someone accused of a mass-murder even knew my name was frightening. But I have to admit I couldn't help wondering about the narrative itself — which read so much like a piece of fiction — about the mysteries behind it. What kind of man was Aiken? Why did he write what he wrote? Who were these others he mentioned? And Carrick, what sort of place was it?

As I said at the start, some of the earlier incidents had been reported widely: the killing and maiming of the shepherd Swainston, for example. I'd already read about that in the newspapers. And I'd heard about the alleged suicide of Kirk, the Colonial, and about the wholesale deaths of animals — a murrain, they were calling it, an animal plague.

But even plague couldn't have spread as quickly as rumours did. The secrecy, the rigour of the quarantine, the involvement of squads of police investigators, the installation of a military barracks, the arrival of teams of medical specialists — all these things had signalled something more deadly than any murrain.

And now I knew what it was. No plague had decimated Carrick, but an awful crime. Aiken, this Robert Aiken who knew my name, was accused of exterminating the population of the town.

I understood that fact, but there were so many other allusions and obscure hints in the document, I needed to read it again. So I did read it for the third time, and only then did I phone Reeve Blair. I came to the point right away.

"Did this pharmacist Robert Aiken really poison them all?"

"He's been charged with it, James."

67

"This thing he wrote — this document — is it supposed to be a confession?"

"I asked him that very question. He said you're the only one he'd give the answer to."

"Why did he want me, in particular? I'd really like to know that."

"It was my fault. He wouldn't tell me anything, but he said he might be persuaded to talk to a newspaper reporter. That's when I mentioned your name. I said I thought he could trust you, James." The Reeve's soft voice was persuasive. "You'd be the only journalist allowed into Carrick. It would be a great opportunity to learn your trade. I couldn't let you file any reports while you were in Carrick, but you'd be able to talk directly to Aiken and the others. And you could write the whole thing up as soon as you got back to the Capital."

"I'd need to speak to my editor."

"I already have. He says it's up to you."

I took one deep breath.

"When do I leave for Carrick?" I asked.

In that brief moment I'd made up my mind. I was fed up with being a student — I felt I'd left enough of my life sleeping in books. I wanted to *do* something for a change. At the same time, I'm sure I was thinking: What a great opportunity! Perhaps I'll be famous!

Now, I wonder if any decision can ever be that simple. I ask myself, does any of us know, really, why we do what we do? That was one of the lessons I was to learn in Carrick.

2

I love to lose myselfe in a mystery,
to pursue my reason to an
o altitudo.

SIR THOMAS BROWNE,
RELIGIO MEDICI, LONDON, 1643

On Sunday the twenty-fifth of March, at one in the afternoon, a camouflaged army jeep (the camouflage made it
look even more conspicuous) picked me up in the Capital
and took me south towards Carrick. I'd brought a small bag
with some changes of clothes, a tape-recorder, tapes, notebooks, Aiken's narrative and a bottle of whisky — strictly
for emergencies; I was only a novice drinker. The day was
fairly bright to begin with, but as we climbed deeper into
the hills the sky turned to lead. After two hours, we arrived
at the outskirts of Carrick and had to slow down to pass a
military roadblock. My driver said something to the armed
sentries and they waved us through.

We drove on into the town and I had a firsthand look at
the Carrick Green and the buildings around it. Soldiers
were posted here and there; I noticed two of them outside
the store with the sign AIKEN'S PHARMACY. The jeep
kept going right on through the town and further east, a
mile or so. We had to drive over an unpaved road full of
potholes till we came to the barracks at the base of
the hills.

I unpacked my things in the room assigned to me in one of the Nissen huts. Then I went to the mess-hall for a cheese sandwich and brought it back to my room. I was at a loose end and feeling a bit nervous, wondering what I was supposed to do next. Around four o'clock, I answered a knock at the door.

"Good-afternoon, James." Reeve Blair was standing outside, looking more than ever like a monk. His grey hair was cut shorter than I remembered; his ascetic appearance fitted well with the cold gloom of the afternoon. "It's good to see you again." His lips lassoed the words in that odd way, as though he didn't wish them to wander too far away.

"Come on in."

"Thank you, no," he said. "Why don't you put on your coat and come with me down to the town? Bring your tape-recorder. You'll be able to find out for yourself what's going on in Carrick. Isn't that what you came here for, James?" Because of that twist of his lips, everything seemed ironic, even the way he said my name, even the word Carrick.

During our walk down to Carrick we talked quite a bit — as we were to do all through my stay there. It was the beginning of a lifelong friendship. If I thought of Reeve Blair then as a sort of a monk, it wasn't because he showed any interest in religion. In fact, during several of our conversations in that week he made it plain to me that matters divine were of little interest to him. I remarked to him one day that he was like one of those old religious cabalists in his attitude to his work.

"Not at all," he said. "Those who follow my profession are concerned with mysteries — not mumbo-jumbo." He might have been a little annoyed at my suggestion, though it was always hard to tell what his moods were — or even if he *had* moods.

I think, too, that he put dreams in the same category as religion. At first, I used to try to tell him about the strange dreams Carrick, or living in Carrick, seemed to bring on in me; but though he listened patiently, I could tell he didn't find them all that interesting.

"For myself," he eventually told me, "I try never to dream. And if I dream in spite of everything, I do my best to forget it."

I was surprised to hear him say this. I'd always believed dreams could be deeply revealing, no matter how puzzling they might appear. I told him so and he shook his head.

"On the contrary," he said. "So far as I'm concerned, dreams are nothing but the garbage of the intellect. They mangle and distort. It's impossible to infer anything meaningful from them."

It seems to me now that this tough-mindedness over certain things may have sprung from his experiences as a child — though I'm sure he wouldn't have agreed with me. ("Avoid simplistic solutions," I imagine him saying. "You can do better than that, James.")

Nevertheless, he did have a difficult childhood. He told

me that during the War, when he was only ten, the Southern industrial city where he lived was bombed in an air raid at night. His parents had taken him and his younger sister to their local bomb-shelter for safety. But his sister began crying, "Lucy! Lucy! I want Lucy!" and they realized they'd left Lucy, the family cat, behind. So his parents told him to look after his sister and they hurried back to their house to look for the animal. They had just gone in the front door when a bomb scored a direct hit. Searchers, after the siren signalled the end of the raid, heard a cat miaowing, and found Lucy under some beams, the only living thing in the smouldering rubble of the house.

Those were hard times for orphans on this Island. The two children (Reeve Blair's sister was seven), having no other relatives, were separated and were committed to state orphanages that were spartan enough even in peacetime. What kind of a life Reeve Blair led in that orphanage during those years till the end of the War and after it, I don't know. He would only say that as soon as he was old enough to leave the orphanage, he was glad to go.

So, what with the loss of his parents and having to spend those formative years in state care, I think he developed his unsentimental view of life and that austere appearance that went with it. Of course he himself was cautious about judging people by appearance and warned me against doing so.

"Believe me, James. In my profession, I've learnt that wealth and success can give an attractive aura to even the most vicious criminals," he said. "And at the same time, their victims are often made ugly by their suffering. There's an irony for you. Ugly people don't get much sympathy."

No doubt he was right about that.

I knew he was sensitive about being a Southerner living and working here in the North. After all, for most of our history, North and South have conducted merciless wars against each other. It's only since we've become allies, especially in these recent Wars, that we've come to rely on each other. So the old hostility hasn't disappeared entirely. Take language, for example. North and South speak the same language, but even our accents seem at odds with each other. Theirs is soft and melodious (effete, we would say), ours is harsh and strong, and we make no effort to change it.

So I wondered why a man from the South, like Reeve Blair, had come to the North of the Island to practise his profession.

"At first it wasn't by choice. I was sent to the Academy here for my training," he said. "But I've come to like the North. I don't know quite how to put it, except that the North's more complicated than the South. Nothing's straightforward here. People keep things hidden, even trivial things, and it's hard to know why — maybe it's just a natural liking for secrecy. In the North real mysteries become even more mysterious."

He'd entered the Academy of the Laws very young, and done well there. He'd advanced through the various ranks of Sentinel at great speed, and become the youngest Reeve ever to head a division of the Ministry of Special Investigations.

The secret of his success? I asked him that one night, and though he didn't answer the question directly, he did say something I thought noteworthy.

"It's a matter of never allowing yourself to be blinded by morality, or even your own sense of decency," he said. "Nothing obstructs the progress of an investigation more than the moral prejudices of a decent man."

Clearly, if being the upholder of some moral standard is a necessary characteristic of a monk, Reeve Blair wasn't any kind of monk at all. But I can't quite give up that image of him. Perhaps, if he was a monk, it was after all only in the sense that he loved to contemplate the mysteries. To that pursuit (and *only* to that, I might once have written), he had dedicated his life.

On that first evening at Carrick we walked together down towards the town, Reeve Blair and I. We didn't take a jeep. The soldiers and all other staff were under orders to walk whenever possible, so as to cut down on pollutants while tests of one sort or another were still being conducted in Carrick.

"We only use vehicles in emergencies," the Reeve said as we walked.

"Emergencies?" I was surprised. "But isn't everything here an emergency? Isn't this whole area in a state of emergency?"

"So a newcomer might think," he said.

He wouldn't expand on that particular remark though I asked him what he meant. He said he wanted me to see for myself what was going on, and make up my own mind about things in Carrick. He was very serious about this, so I left the subject alone.

We went down to the town in the dusk, chatting about this and that. The eastern sky was in total darkness; but away to the west, a slow-motion battle was going on between the massed night and the red horizon.

"What a sky," I said. "It's beautiful."

"That's a word you won't hear often in Carrick," he said.

We reached the town in about twenty minutes and turned left at the Green. I couldn't help glancing over to the north side, towards the Pharmacy where the guards were still standing at the door. A light was shining in the upstairs rooms.

"Is that somebody at the window above the Pharmacy?"

"Doubtless," Reeve Blair said, but he didn't look.

At the building with the unlit CAFE sign over it, the Reeve pushed the door open and we went inside. The place was deserted. The tabletops bristled with chair legs, and the glass display counter gleamed emptily. On the main wall I could see a painting of a dark landscape and squat hills — perhaps the same hills I'd seen on the way up to the barracks. The cafe had that stale after-smell of eating places that have been closed for a long time.

And there was another smell, a faint one I couldn't pin down.

The Reeve headed towards the stairs at the rear.

"This way. We're going up to visit Kennedy. I'll warn you of one thing: the poison has affected his speech, and now he says everything backwards. Even if you don't understand him, just pretend you do." Then, just as we were about to start up the stairs, he said: "One more thing. We'll only stay a few minutes. His wife died two days ago and he doesn't have long to live."

I didn't like the sound of that, but I was here now and what was there to do but climb the stairs after him? At the top, in a comfortable room, two men were bent over a table full of test-tubes. They looked like grown-up twins in their identical gowns and surgical masks. Behind them through the open curtains, I could see the Green outlined in the street lamps. One of the men looked up, and his lips moved behind the mask.

"Don't take too long. We'll be doing more tests soon."

That odd smell I'd noticed before was even more noticeable up here, and a little more acrid. A man's voice came from the room on the left; as we went towards it I could tell this was the source of the smell. Inside, an elderly woman with a lined face and a white nurse's cap over blue rinsed hair was fussing around the bed. She paid no attention to us for she was listening to the man in the bed who was leaning back with his arms folded behind his head, talking. His thick, black hair was combed down the middle of his head, and a shrubbery of black hair stuck through the placket of his pyjamas. He looked round and saw us. He narrowed his dark eyes at the sight of the Reeve, but he smiled at me as I took my tape-recorder out of my pocket and switched it on.

"Me see and come to you of nice," he said to me.

This was Kennedy. His voice was strong and he certainly didn't look like a dying man.

"He's just been telling me about his wife's twin sister," said the nurse. "He says it's the first time he's told anyone about her. Isn't that so?"

"Yes oh. Girl a quite was she," Kennedy said. "Them loved she and her loved family her." He seemed quite unaware of the inversion in his speech. "Birth at bat a as blind was she. See could she and eyes her on operation an did Capital the in hospital a at doctors the, twelve was she when." (*I was having trouble understanding him now. What follows is the transcription of his words I made later from my tape.*) "But she didn't like being able to see. She couldn't even stand the sight of my wife who'd always been her best friend and was her double. She said her dog was the only creature that looked as nice as she'd expected things to look, except for shadows. She liked shadows. My wife and the others coaxed her to look at herself in the mirror; but she said she knew she'd hate the sight of herself as much as she hated the sight of her sister, and she wouldn't look. Most of the time, she was content to sit in her room with the lights out, stroking the dog. After a month, she poked a knitting needle into both her eyes. They bandaged her up and she was happy again. She was happy as a queen."

Kennedy nodded his head up and down, up and down, still looking at me; and I, I suppose, nodded mine, though

I'd only half understood much of what he'd just said. The Reeve cut into our exchange of nodding.

"And how about you, Kennedy? How do you feel yourself?" His voice was at its most gentle.

Kennedy still ignored him and spoke to me.

"Not bad at all, for a dying man."

It was hard for me to believe that this hearty, talkative man was ill, never mind doomed, even though he did have that symptomatic oddity in his speech.

The two doctors came into the room just at that moment and Kennedy switched his attention to them.

"Would you like to hear about my wife's twin sister?" With great gusto, he began his story again. The Reeve and I left discreetly and if Kennedy noticed, he didn't give any sign. He seemed to care only about having a fresh audience for his monologue. He was even using the very same phrases: "bat a as blind" and "shadows for except."

Going downstairs, I noticed that the fainter his voice became, the more diluted was that pungent smell, till it disappeared when we stepped outside into the cold, fresh air. Across the Green to the west, the darkness was complete as we began walking back to the barracks.

"Are you all right, James?" The Reeve's voice was anxious. "Some find it hard to be with people so close to death."

"I was a bit worried at first. But he doesn't look at all as though he's dying. In fact, I can still hardly believe it. Why did he speak to me all the time? Why did he ignore you? Doesn't he like policemen?"

"No, that's not what it is. I'm from the South," he said. "It's as simple as that." He was silent after he said it, and

I couldn't see his face. I thought it might be wiser to change the subject.

"Do you have any idea what the poison is?"

"Yes, I do," the Reeve said. "Last week when I was in the Capital, the Chief Medical Officer told me about it."

"One mystery's solved," said the Chief Medical Officer, a small man with a belly almost bursting the buttons on his striped suit so that it appeared he had a balloon in there. He was a neat man, too, with his tie tied precisely, and he made Reeve Blair feel huge and unkempt. "The poison is the effect of a bacterium. That is absolutely certain. But, you ask me, which bacterium?" He talked as though he were giving an introductory lecture to his pathology students. "Ah yes, that's quite another problem. Bacteria are uncommonly hard to pin down; they live in soil, water, or air, even fire. They inhabit the four elements. They can be parasites on human beings or animals or plants. In short, they are everywhere."

The two men were sitting in a restaurant under the brow of the Castle. The Chief Medical Officer was examining the face of Reeve Blair shrewdly as though the bacterium in question might be lurking there.

"This particular strain that's on the loose in Carrick evidently produces an exotoxia that's deadly. The symptoms are quite peculiar: the toxin insinuates itself into the nervous system and causes a diplegia, especially in the legs." The Chief Medical Officer leaned forward, confiding in Reeve Blair. "But, most curiously of all, this bacterium brings about a kind of aphasia which has no parallel in the literature of medical science. The victims seem to suffer from a variety of speech irregularities. But the most remarkable symptom of the aphasia is the way it makes them garrulous. All they seem to want to do is talk, talk, talk, till they die."

Reeve Blair who had been unable to interject a word so far, kept a serious look on his face.

"As a sort of compensation for their infirmity," the Chief Medical Officer continued, "the victims apparently feel a great sense of euphoria for most of the time — a kind of blissfulness. The males in particular rarely show concern for their impending deaths, though they seem fully aware that death is inevitable. Some of our researchers say this euphoria is highly dangerous, because it discourages the body's defence mechanisms from fighting off the toxin." He reached for the menu. "I hope all of this isn't too technical for you, Blair. The long and short of it is that this poison is a killer, but a very benign killer."

Then he began to study the entrées.

"A benign killer," the Reeve said as we walked. "That's the phrase he used. He said if he could bottle it and distribute it around the globe, it would be the greatest medical advance of the century. But not good for business."

We reached the gate of the barracks and walked right past Reeve Blair's room in the first Nissen hut, towards my hut near the back of the compound. When I could see his face and his grey eyes quite plainly under the light of the bulb over my door, I asked him again about a matter that was still troubling me.

"Reeve Blair. Why am I here in Carrick, really?"

"Here are the facts, James," he said. "Our investigation was getting nowhere and the townspeople were all dying. Aiken's written account was vague and enigmatic, and he wouldn't say anything more. Except that he might be willing to talk to someone he could trust — a reporter. I remembered you from the banquet, and I thought we might help each other."

"But why did you charge him with the poisoning in the first place? In his account he blames Kirk for everything."

"There was cirmcumstantial evidence. A lot of it. Add to that the fact that everyone else was dying except for him. When he was charged, he just laughed. He didn't deny any part of it."

"But why would he poison all his friends? Does that make any sense?" (These were questions I was to ask over and over again at Carrick.)

"I hope you'll find the answers, James." His voice was urgent. "This is one case where I absolutely need to know as much as can humanly be known."

Just before he turned away, he reached into his coat pocket and pulled out a manilla envelope. "I almost forgot," he said. "Aiken asked me to give you this — for your evening's reading."

He left, and I went inside. It was good to be out of the cold air. I sat down at the table under the glare of the ceiling light. "AIKEN'S PHARMACY" was stamped on the left top corner of the envelope. It wasn't sealed. I took out the contents — several pages torn from an old book. The first was a title-page:

VOLUME X
of the author's
WORKS
containing
TRAVELLS
into severall remote partes of
THIS ILAND
by
Johannes Peregrinus

certum quia impossibile

Printed for J. Thynne and are to be solde
at his shoppe in Castle Close Alley
and by S. Wallis at the
Stagge Inne
1660

I read the attached pages — they seemed to have been ripped out of the same book:

I attended, in that yeere, the annual Festival of the Mysterium at Carricke, a rare wonder. The feesting lastes for fyve dayes. On the firste daye, craftesmen from all over this Iland assemble in a great processional. Eech crafte or mystery is represented by a master and an apprentice. The Heade of the Council of Carricke beares before them the keyes of the towne as they marche. The craftes dresse alle in their livery eche according to its kinde, and the apprentice carries the escutcheons of theyre gild. Here is the banner of the goldesmith with his bauble, the fishmonger with his smelle, the mercer with his silke, the vintner with his tunne, *the apothecary with his pestle*, the man of lawe with his irons, the baker with his loafe, the painter with his brushe, the mason with his stone, the cutler with his wheele, the barber-surgeon with his sawe, the armorer with his halberd, the carpenter with his plumbe, the tailor with his effigie, the shoemaker with his laste, the skinner with his furs, the fuller with his webbe, the ironmonger with his pottes, the smiddy with his bellowes, the butcher with his hacckse, the spurrier with his spikes, the draper with his cloath, the sheathmaker with his scabbarde, the girdler with his belte, the weavere with his loom, the chandler with his tallowe, the brewere with his bottle. And so they passe with theyre banneres, the stirruppe maker, the joinere, the fruiterere, the dealer in burddes, the glovver, the pouche makker, the hostelere, the cooke, the collector of antiquities, the librariane, the bookesellere, the physician, the cordewainer.

When those various mysteries reeche the Greene of Carricke, they assemble together and make their oth at the Carricke Churche:

Wee swear that we will well and truly oversee our mysteries. And all good rules and ordinances we shall keepe. And all the errours we find done in those same craftes we shall punish, sparing no man for favour nor harming no persoun for hate. And we shall preserve eech crafte the other against alle such enemies as appere amonst us. So help us alle the saintes.

After that ceremony at the Greene, the Festival continues fyve dayyes with much drinking and eating and wenching. On the thirde daye, they performe thayre stayge-playye of the *Mysterium Mysteriorum* — the Mystery of Mysteries. Onely initiates may witnesse it on payne of deathe. For the remaynder of that Festival, the villagers and towns-people from alle the country around come there to Carricke, as well as those of the wicked sorte, the ruffleres, priggeres, pransers, palliards, fraters, whip-jacks, swadders, and jarkemen. Stille worse, for they carry their deseases with them, bawdy-baskets, walking mortes, doxies, and kinching cooes.

This Festival has occurred at Carricke for as farre back as men may remember. Some say, it began there when the ancient walle that divides that parte of the Iland was builded.

At the ende of the fifthe day, I must continue my travells. I tolde the Carricke towne apothecary in his shoppe my affliction, all my life, with a sleep-lessness conducive to a melancholy. That wise man, experte in his mystery, gave me this preparation whereby I might sleepe atte laste: Take equal quan-tities of seed of henbane, darnel, black poppy, and dried briory rootes; pound it together in a brass mor-tar very fine; you shall sleepe less or more, even unto dethe, according to the amount taken.

I have found it, gentle reader, a sovereign remedy.

Many of the words on these pages were unknown to me though I understood the general sense. The oath had been underlined in ink. Otherwise, I didn't quite know what to make of the passage — I'd need Reeve Blair's opinion on that.

Later, I transcribed the tape of Kennedy's monologue, reversing the order of the words; then, about midnight, I undressed for bed. I switched off the light and looked out the window. The night was foggy now and rain was falling, but so lightly it only whispered to the roof. In the direction where the Cairn lay, I thought for a moment I saw something move beyond the perimeter fence of the barracks. But if there was something, it was so grey it blended in with the greyness of the fog. I stared and stared till my eyes were weary from trying to penetrate the impenetrable, then I gave up and went to bed.

I woke early on Monday, March the twenty-sixth, to my first full day in Carrick — a foggy, wet day. Around eight-thirty, I took some coffee and toast in the mess-hall then went back to my room, put on my heavy sweater and yellow slicker and started down to the village. The Reeve had suggested that today I look over some of the places Aiken had mentioned in his narrative: the scenes of the crimes. Or of THE crime. So I spent the rainy morning visiting the Monument, the Library, The Stag, the Keep, the railway station and the graveyard. I knew them well enough from Aiken's descriptions to feel as though I were coming back to a place I had once lived in.

Last on my itinerary was Swainston's cottage, which I

reached around noon. By then, I was thankful for my yellow slicker. The rain was heavier: in the exposed areas up in the moorlands, it was hard enough to flatten the bracken.

As I approached the cottage, I could still see the red circular smear on the eastern gable: the Carrick weather hadn't managed yet to wipe it off completely. I went round to the south-west side, where the stone dyke runs back to some sheep pens. The place where the dead man had been propped up was easy to find. The outline of his body, in faded yellow police chalk, was there on the wall.

The attack began while I was standing looking at the wall.

I'd pulled the hood of my slicker back a little from my face when a squawk right above my head startled me; then claws — long black claws — scrabbled at my forehead and my eyes. My attacker was a heavy black bird. I covered my face with my left arm, and swatted at the bird with my right; but even though I struck its wings at least twice, it kept coming back at me — I could even smell its acrid bird-smell. Then my fist caught it right on the beak and it arched away, screaming abuse at me, and flapped off to the east.

The skin of my left hand was broken and my forehead too; when I touched it I saw blood on my fingers. As fast as I could, I made my way back down to the barracks. I kept my arm up, ready to defend my head in case the bird came back at me silently.

I got to the barracks shortly after one o'clock. The young nurse who bathed the scratches shook her head when I told her about the bird. She was a dour-faced woman but talkative. She said she'd been brought up in a hill town just like Carrick.

"Didn't anyone warn you to be careful of the birds?" she asked. "Even children up here learn not to be too trusting."

While she dabbed on the iodine, she talked knowledgeably about the moor-birds. During salmon runs, she said, the birds would sit on rocks and peck out the eyes of the poor, sex-crazed fish. Those salmon would leap in the air as sighted creatures, and land in the water, a second later, blind. Some of the black moor-birds, she said, liked bigger prey than fish, and had a habit of blinding lambs. "And they've been known to attack human beings. A stranger should know these things before wandering around the hills," she said. Then she remarked, as an afterthought: "Some people say the blind lambs stay tender and make the best eating, the way blinded songbirds sing best. It seems the loss of one faculty improves another."

After dinner I dressed myself quite carefully for the first interview Reeve Blair had arranged for me. From reading Aiken's narrative, I was very curious about the townspeople I was to meet. I knew they all had one thing in common: they were dying; but I felt I could cope with that since my experience at Kennedy's.

Around five o'clock I made my way down to Carrick. The evening was fogless and rainless; but it was very cold. When I reached the town, I went to the antique store, and pushed the door open. The clapper jangled in its brass skull. A nurse in a black cape was waiting for me just inside the door. She was the same one I'd seen at Kennedy's, a woman with rinsed hair. In the dim light of the store, with her lined face, she might have been mistaken for one of the antiques.

She told me I was expected. She would take the opportunity to go up to the barracks for a quick dinner: "I'll be back in an hour and a half." She pointed to the curtain at the end of the centre aisle. "She's up there." Then she went out into the night.

I took a look around the store and saw a lot of the objects Aiken had noted: the bagpipes, the photo albums, the old books, the tailor's dummies, the plaster elephants, the glass cases of moths and leaves. And I couldn't help noticing some things he'd neglected to mention (perhaps they were recent additions): a colourful painting of a tropical marketplace full of hundreds of identical-looking people; a woodcarving of what seemed like two naked, intertwined lovers, but close up was really a swirling mass of snakes; a collection of bronze burial urns with indecipherable inscriptions; and a wall poster showing various knots. One was called "The Carrick Bend."

As I walked to the back of the store, I couldn't help noticing a pungent smell that was stronger than the fusty aroma of all those antiques; it was the same smell that had permeated Kennedy's cafe. Not even the perfume that clung to the blue curtain at the back of Anna's store did much to combat it.

I pushed the curtain aside, took a deep breath, and

climbed the creaky stairs. The bannister was smooth in my right hand.

The room at the top of the stairs was warmer than any place I'd been all day: a coal fire glowed in an old-fashioned range. A table lamp lit up a sofa and a stuffed armchair and other unremarkable furniture. A picture of an elderly couple and a small girl hung over a low bookcase. Dark blue curtains covered the window that looked out on the Green.

To my left, through an open door, I could see the bottom of a bed with a red blanket and the hillock made by feet under it. I could also hear a woman's voice talking quietly.

I cleared my throat.

"Anybody home?"

"Come in," said the voice, so I went into the bedroom, expecting to see both the owner of the voice and the person she'd been speaking to.

But Anna Grubach was quite alone. She was propped up against two thick pillows in a bed with a carved, dark wooden frame. It was hard to tell her age, though according to Reeve Blair she was in her forties. She was certainly pleasant to look at. Her fair hair was long, combed back from her wide forehead. She was wearing a green nightdress with a neckline low enough to show heavy breasts. Clearly she wasn't a small woman.

The furniture in the bedroom — the plush chair by the bed, the elegant bedside table, the armoire with books and papers on it, the glass-doored bookcase, the ornate, full-length mirror on the wall beside the bed — looked antique.

Anna's green eyes were examining me. Mascara didn't disguise their astuteness. Her voice was deeper, more throaty than I'd expected.

"Well, well. So you're young Maxwell. I hope that Southern policeman made a good choice. Take off your coat and sit down." Her face was powder white and her lips were bright red, as though she'd just put on lipstick. She didn't look ill, but like a woman who'd just decided to take a rest. I felt uncomfortable because of the intimacy as much as from the heat: here I was in this upper room, the special guest of a freshly made-up stranger already in bed in her nightdress.

But dying. I mustn't forget that.

She was studying the scratches on my face as I sat down and started my tape-recorder.

"I see you've already met some of our wildlife," she said. "I'm so sorry. Sorry. Sorry." And suddenly she began to weep, pointing at my scratches, convulsing with sobs, saying over and over, "Sorry, sorry, I'm so sorry."

I was shocked, even though I was prepared for her outburst — Reeve Blair had warned me this was the way the poison showed itself in Anna: she'd become the victim of certain words. That is to say, some key words seemed to trigger off great spasms of emotion in her. Her moods were utterly fragile, as though protected only by the flimsiest of eggshells. I took the Reeve's advice and pretended I didn't notice her display of feeling, though it was genuine and upsetting to me.

After a while, she stopped crying and wiped her eyes.

"That was good," she said, quite under control again. She gestured in the direction of the armoire: "I keep a bottle of whisky over there. Help yourself."

Without thinking, I said no — and her mood changed instantly. Now she was livid.

"How dare you refuse! Get out of here! Get out of here!" She was shrieking this at me, and clearly meant it.

Again, I followed Reeve Blair's advice. I pretended to pay no attention to her screams. I said on second thought I would take a drink and I crossed over to the armoire. The bundle of paper on the top was a copy of Aiken's narrative. I moved it aside very deliberately, lifted the bottle of Old Mortality and poured myself some. I put the bottle back, went over to my chair again and sat down.

Anna's anger evaporated, and she sighed.

"That was so good," she said. Then, "You've read it?"

These sudden changes in her moods were disconcerting, and it took me a moment to realize she was referring to Aiken's account.

"What did you think of his Anna?" She put this to me as though she were inquiring about someone else, a character in a book, not herself. I tried to think of something safe to say, so as not to set her off again.

"She was interesting."

It was the right phrase, and she seemed content.

"Yes. She was indeed interesting. All things considered."

As she said this, I noticed something the Reeve hadn't told me about: her facial expression and her voice weren't quite synchronized — the way sometimes in a film the sound-track anticipates the movement of the actors' lips. Anna's frowns, her smiles, the widening or narrowing of her eyes would occur a second after the words they should have accompanied. All her gestures were a shade too late. Her mind seemed to be one move ahead of her body — art anticipating nature.

"There are certain things I must tell you about Robert Aiken, and about his father, Alexander Aiken, and about Kirk," she said. She looked in the mirror. "I'll begin with Robert. Did you know he was my first love? We were very young. Can you imagine, how it felt to be in love so young?"

That was how she began. For most of the next hour, I sat and listened, fascinated by her account and by wild fluctuations in her moods that she seemed to take so much pleasure in. As she talked, she constantly examined herself in the mirror by the bed, patting her hair with her fingertips, looking herself over as though she were unused to the sight of herself. But she may have been trying to figure out some way of synchronizing her words and her gestures.

THE TESTIMONY OF ANNA GRUBACH

(transcribed from tape and compressed by me, James Maxwell)

They played together when they were children, little Anna and little Robert. By the time they were fourteen, their friendship had ripened considerably. So, after school one day, knowing exactly what they meant to do, they walked up into the moors, and climbed the

Monolith. Stretched out on the soft moss on top, they began their usual exploration of each other's bodies with all the sweet delirium of adolescence. She knew he wanted her to say, "I love you." But she could not. She had no wish to express such emotions in words.

So they did not talk much. But on that day, up there on the Monolith, they experimented with a manoeuvre they had never tried before. Though the results were immediate and astonishing they presumed their awkward gymnastics were a kind of an apprenticeship, not knowing they had it right, first time.

After that, every day, they worked at perfecting it; it (Anna regarded "it" as love) became their favourite pastime. At school she would send him messages, unspoken messages that passed from mind directly to body. Words themselves were useless to her. When she tried to articulate what she felt, even when she was alone, the words perished from exposure to the air. She tried writing poems but that was no good; the words on paper seemed to flare up out of control and burn her, their creator.

So, wordlessly, each day after school, she would go with him to the Monolith. She felt they were the only waking beings in a world of sleepwalkers. As soon as they were out of sight of Carrick they could not stop touching each other, as though love had made their hands into magnets. All day, desire had sated their minds; now their bodies were bursting with need.

On top of the Monolith they would undress and then they would wrestle frenziedly, so that an innocent watching them might have thought they were enemies. After they had made love, they would climb back down, adjust their clothing carefully, then walk back to the town, full of the smells and tastes of each other, the after-images of their nakedness.

THEY WERE LOVERS all through that period of their growing up. Then they were no longer lovers. Then they became friends.

And so the years passed. The elder Aiken — Alexander — was taken to an asylum on the edge of the north woods, carrying only one bag — his madness. He was there for five years, his only visitor Robert. One day when Anna was at work in her store Robert came to her and begged her to accompany him on a visit to his father. She, for friendship's sake, agreed to do so.

They caught the Friday morning train from Carrick to the Capital, sharing their compartment with the clammy smells of fifty years of coal smoke, tobacco smoke and the compressed spoors of generations of travellers.

"These accumulations of smells, Robert," Anna said, seeing the tension in him, "they're how a dog understands history, don't you think?"

Robert Aiken did not smile, so she kept quiet after that.

In two hours, the train reached the outskirts of the Capital. As they rattled past disused factories and run-down warehouses, Anna had the sensation of entering a huge carious mouth. And of leaving it again. For after they got out of the train in the Eastern Station, they had to take a taxi the rest of the way.

About twenty silent miles north of the Capital, the northern forest stretched a tentative paw which had been penetrated by a splinter of rough road. Heavy rain obscured visibility but the taxi charged heavily along this narrow road, making Anna apprehensive as the forest funnelled past them. At one point, the driver braked suddenly and pulled off onto the narrow shoulder. A black van slithered past them with MINISTRY OF INSTITUTIONS on its side panel; she caught a glimpse of the driver's flat face.

They drove on for perhaps another mile till the sky became lighter, the rain slacker. On their right appeared the sign REGIONAL ASYLUM. The taxi turned up a long driveway, stopping at a security post for clearance before cruising slowly past extensive lawns bordered by an electrified fence. The lawns were all at the front; the rear was the domain of the forest. The building itself, built as a private house two hundred years before, bristled with chimneys and turrets; many of the ornate windows were bricked over, others were barred — the daydreams of one era so easily transformed into the nightmares of another.

Anna waited while Robert arranged with the taxi-driver for the return trip, then together they climbed the worn steps to the heavy doors. The guard, a friendly man, recognized Robert:

"I hope your father's feeling better today," he said. He switched on an intercom, announced their arrival and let them into the lobby to sit and wait.

While they waited, the guard told Anna about the asylum and the patients. He seemed to take a personal pride in many of them: the two sisters who had scourged and mutilated their own elderly parents for thirty years; the physician from a hospital in the northern islands who exchanged the organs of two of his male patients, sewing an infected appendix into one and a diseased testicle into the other; a woman with a dangerously split personality who was actually found to have two hearts and a different pulse rate in each wrist.

Anna did not much like the waiting or the guard's conversation, but she knew they needed a warden to lead them to Alexander's room, for the asylum was labyrinthine and the doors were not numbered. Robert had once told her of patients who managed to break open the doors of their rooms at night when all the lights were off; the escapees only managed to find their way, madder than ever, to the centre of that dark maze.

In due course the guard left and a tall, black-haired woman came into the lobby — their warden. The corners of her sad mouth were lipsticked into an upward, smiling flourish matched by upturned wings of eye-shadow at the edges of her dark eyes. Robert asked how his father was feeling, and she smiled (she could do nothing else but smile): "That will be for you to judge," she said.

She led them along intricate corridors past many doors through which they could hear moans and sobs, then she stopped at a door that looked like all the others. She turned her key in the lock and opened the door, setting free the pent-up smell of urine and foul air. Anna and Robert took a last breath of the disinfected air of the corridor and went inside.

The door slammed shut behind them, the key turned in the lock and the warder's footsteps receded. Alexander lay on his side on a small bunk, glaring at them.

"How are you?" Robert asked nervously; Anna knew his father would never have answered such a question even when he was well. His old man's body seemed to her as delicate as a chrysalis, the veins pulsing visibly as though his life would soon shuffle free, leaving only a tangle of dry skin behind. But something still fuelled his eyes, something unpleasant.

Robert reached out to put a hand on his shoulder in a filial way, but Alexander shrank back and slapped at the hand as though it were a wasp.

"Leave me alone! I don't want to die!" His voice was shrill but strong for such a feeble body. "I wasn't the only one. It isn't fair." Tears were finding a route down the wrinkles in his cheeks.

"Now, now." Robert tried to squeeze the shrivelled hand. "Everything's all right."

"Don't touch me! Don't touch me!" the old man screeched, swatting the hand away again.

Anna, who had said nothing, moved forward to console him; but Alexander looked at her with such venom from behind his veil of madness that Robert reached over and held her back.

The old man wept again:

"Don't let them cremate me," he said. "The oven makes the intestines shrink and the body sits up. I couldn't bear it."

This might have been laughable, Anna thought, if he had not been so sad and so desperate. The mad eyes turned to her.

"We'll kill them all. Did he tell you that?" He was full of glee in spite of the tears streaming down his face.

"What do you think of that, eh? Every single one of them."

He went on in this mixture of boasting and malice that was not pleasant to watch. Suddenly his face wrinkled like a baby's and he sobbed: "It's not fair, it's not fair." For a while he wept noisily at the thought of whatever the injustice was. He seemed unaware now of the presence of his visitors. He turned away from them and hunched into the fetal position. He lay there, Anna thought, waiting to be reborn into that wall of blankness.

They heard an abrupt knock at the door, and the key in the lock. The smiling warden looked in.

"Do you want to stay any longer?"

Robert seemed relieved to see her, and shook his head. "Father," he said, "we have to go now. I'll come back and see you soon."

The lank, grey hair did not move on the pillow.

"Goodbye," Anna said.

There was a slight tensing of the back, no more. And that was the end of the visit. Anna was happy to escape into the corridor. But after the door was locked behind them, she confronted the warden.

"The smell was so bad in there. Isn't there something you can do about it?"

"Smell? I didn't notice any smell." The painted smile was at war with the sad contour of the lips.

The warden led them back along those bewildering corridors, up and down one identical flight of stairs after another, till suddenly they were back in the lobby. They went outside into the clean air and the rain, which was falling heavily again. They said goodbye to the friendly guard and walked to where their taxi waited. Robert was apologetic.

"That wasn't one of his better days."

They had almost reached the taxi, and she felt the need to do something to comfort him. She would have liked to take his hand in her own and press it, but she did not.

"Poor Robert," was all she could say.

The taxi-driver had been smoking and reading a newspaper. When they climbed in, he turned and shut the connecting window which had been slightly open on the journey to the asylum. He shut it with a snap, as though whatever madness they had just encountered might be contagious.

The drive back to the Capital was a silent one, the taxi soothing away the road like balm. They arrived at the Eastern Station in good time for their train and were soon steaming towards Carrick. Anna took the window seat facing the front and watched the engine advance like some great device stitching together a wound on the body of the earth. When the train began its slow climb into the Uplands, a fog blanked out the landscape. Robert was dozing, and Anna, filled with weariness, longed for sleep to come and wipe out consciousness the way the fog had erased the hills. And she did sleep, but only intermittently. She wished she were home in her bed and not in this uncomfortable seat, for she kept waking; and each time she woke, though the hills remained invisible, her memories were clear and substantial as ever.

WITHIN A YEAR of that visit, Martin Kirk, the Colonial, appeared in Carrick. The first night she and

Robert met him in The Stag, she watched his every move. She sensed that he liked her, and she liked the way his Colonial accent transformed words, took the roughness out of them and even made the things the words referred to seem easier to bear.

A few nights later, she met him again in The Stag; this time she was alone with him. They talked for hours. After she had told him about how she and Robert had once been lovers, he told her about his first love.

HE, KIRK, WAS ONLY TWENTY then, an apprentice at his profession, when he was sent to one of those jungle republics to test the water table. The rivers entranced him. Unlike the Colony where cold, killing streams poured northward into frigid seas, each of these tropical rivers was a soup of minute living things. Even his dreams became exotic and vivid, as though the heat fertilized a part of his mind that had hitherto been dormant.

During his stay he and his research assistant, a local woman assigned to him by the government, spent much of each day and night alone together in the jungle. When he made love to the woman, which in time he did, he told her that when his work was over, he would take her back with him to the Colony and she would live a life she could never have imagined. She was a quiet woman and she listened to him and watched him out of dark, Indian eyes.

One morning, they were deep in the jungle taking samples of the water table when a dozen men in tattered uniforms crashed out of the undergrowth and covered them with machine-guns. Two of them held Kirk to one side at gunpoint while the others seized his assistant and ripped the blouse and pants off her. Her eyes took on the glassy sheen of a trapped rabbit. The soldiers spread-eagled her naked body (the soft body Kirk had caressed each night for a month) on the putrid jungle floor. He could do nothing but watch while they took turns raping her.

But they were not finished. Four of them held her still while their leader, a plump man with a jovial smile, forced her eyelids open and poured in cigarette lighter fluid. Then, with a flourish, he ignited it. He allowed her to moan in anguish for a few minutes. Then he unholstered a pearl-handled pistol, bent over her and shot her in the head.

Finally, the leader came over to Kirk. He held the end of the pistol barrel, still hot, against Kirk's temple.

"Click!" he said, laughing. He slid the pistol back in its holster, organized the soldiers, and together they filed away into the bush, not even bothering to look back at Kirk, who was quite unhurt except for that circular mark from the pistol barrel, a stigmata that took months to fade.

ANNA WAS SHOCKED at Kirk's story.

"How awful," she had said.

"I knew then that hell doesn't last forever," Kirk had replied. "It lasts only half an hour, then you have to come back and face the world again. And I learnt another great lesson that day," he had said. "Even if I'd had a gun, I wouldn't have used it on the soldiers. I understood then that a man who can't kill, can't love."

"Could you kill now?" Anna asked him.

"The moment a man learns to love, he learns to kill," he told her.

SHE ASKED KIRK TO COME and visit her at her store. When he came, one afternoon, she latched the door and put the CLOSED sign in the window. She led him up to her rooms. At the top of the stairs, she put her arms around him and kissed him for the first time.

She took his hand and guided him into the bedroom. While they undressed she watched him carefully, how he tried not to appear too impatient for her. When they lay down, she inspected his solid, wiry body, noted the residue of sun on his skin, even in winter. She, in turn, lay back to let him inspect her, adore her with his hands. She helped him slide himself inside her, and she moved rhythmically with him till he arched and groaned, his blue eyes concentrated on extracting pure pleasure out of himself.

She endured his sudden heaviness, his return to awareness of her. He lay back and she ran her hand over his chest and belly.

"Now, rest, Martin Kirk," she said. "We have all day."

"Yes, Maxwell. All day," she repeated.

She was finished. In the telling of her story, she had lost her self-control at times and expressed in her whole body the extremes of sorrow and fear. When she was remembering her love for Aiken and later for Kirk, her right hand slid low under the blankets and her green eyes shone.

"Yes, Maxwell," she said again. "In this bed, I've made love many times." She raised herself on the pillows and I couldn't help noticing how the neck of her nightgown slipped to show more of her breasts.

"Kirk at that time appeared to me," she said, "to be a man capable of falling in love." She was watching my reflection in the mirror by her bed. "Isn't that a rare quality in a man?"

I expected bitterness in her after she said that, and she didn't let me down. The green eyes became slits.

"Men! Take a look at yourself, Maxwell. You'd like to climb in beside me, wouldn't you? You'd be quite willing to make love to a dying woman, wouldn't you? Really. I sometimes wonder if any man is more than a bag of semen with vocal chords."

She spat this out, then turned round from the mirror and looked directly at me. I didn't know what to say. I knew how obvious my mind must be to her. But her mood changed again.

"That was good," she said, and went on: "Robert never liked Kirk. He suspected from the start that he had a darker side. And Robert is always very astute in the matter of darkness."

I was puzzled. "But Aiken's the poisoner — not Kirk." I couldn't understand her lack of animosity towards Aiken.

"Yes, of course. We should have known that. It's always hard to tell what's going on in Robert's mind. He's like a stick in water. Is he bent, or is he not?"

I braced myself. Surely this time there would be an outburst aimed at Aiken; but again she didn't seem at all upset or angry, so I risked another question.

"What would Aiken's motive be for doing such an awful thing?" I asked. "Why would he want to kill all his friends?"

Anna frowned at the mirror.

"Motives. Do you really believe in such things as motives, causes and effects? Do you believe the loose ends can ever be tied up, except in books and plays?" She turned to me and her face became very solemn; her marvellous green eyes looked right into me for a moment. Then she smiled.

"Good heavens. I think you really do. In that case, you'll be interested in what Sentinel Hogg has to tell you about the prisoners."

"Prisoners?"

All of a sudden she looked very tired and seemed to shrink in size as people do who are ill, or near to death. She closed her eyes, shutting me out.

"I'm afraid I can't say any more," she said.

I rose and slowly put on my coat.

Her eyes were closed, but I saw tears trickling from them. In spite of what she'd just said, she did speak again, slowly and clearly.

"I think, Maxwell, we only have a limited portion of loving in us. If we meet the right person in time, we have enough love to give. I'm afraid I frittered most of mine away. By the time I met Kirk, it was too late for me to be happy."

Her voice was sad, but the very word "happy" triggered off another emotion in her. She opened her eyes, blinked away the tears and seemed revitalized, exuberant.

"Oh, that was good," she said. "By the way, Robert did portray me very satisfactorily, didn't he? Can I rely on you to do the same, Maxwell? What will you say? That I was worth meeting?" She looked more beautiful to me than ever. "That I was bad?" Her face was immediately transformed by that word into an embodiment of corruption. She was watching it in the mirror, so I looked there too and answered.

"I'll do the best I can to tell the truth."

The evil image grinned, then the other Anna replaced it, smiling a slow, wonderful smile.

"Truth? Telling truth is only possible when you don't know very much," she said. For once, at least so it seemed to me, her words and her facial expression had been synchronized perfectly.

The nurse arrived just at that moment, and ended the interview. I asked Anna if I could come back and visit her another time.

"I have no more time, Maxwell, don't you realize that? My life is over. I've just reached the age when I can touch the other side of my life — and it's over. My life is over."

She yawned, and seemed weary rather than unhappy. So I went down the dark staircase into the shop. I was beginning, I think, to understand what Reeve Blair had said about these townspeople: they were involved in a deadly race; the quantum of words in them was quickly emptying itself, using itself up — and their lives were running out with it.

I stepped out into the street and closed the door of the antique store behind me along with the pungent smell. I must have been very impressionable that night, for the Green seemed to me like a great black pit, with Carrick perched unsteadily on its rim. I skirted the abyss and hurried back to the safety of the barracks.

In the sanity of my room again, I began to wonder how much I could trust Anna Grubach. Even if her facts were accurate, surely her judgment was distorted, her mind warped by the poison. She had said she believed in a world where motive and cause and effect weren't important, where truth was impossible to tell, where resolutions could only be found in books and plays!

I couldn't accept that. I myself wanted certainties. How else could a person survive? And yet an image kept surfacing in my mind — that Carrick itself really was a theatre of some kind, and that I'd half-knowingly wandered into it; that some intricate performance was either about to begin, or was already under way; that I was part-audience and part-actor.

I had managed to put that idea out of my head and was puzzling over Anna's lack of hostility towards Aiken (her one-time lover now her murderer), when there was a knock at the door. Reeve Blair came in with a black leather brief-case under his arm.

"So one of the moor-birds got you." He had noticed the claw-marks on my face.

I ran the tips of my fingers over the braille of the scratches, and told him how my day's walking tour had ended with the savage encounter at Swainston's cottage.

"And how was your visit to Anna Grubach?"

I remembered the green eyes, the breasts, the body squirming as she talked of her loves.

"I like her. She's a very unusual woman."

"Quite."

I played him the tape of the interview and he sat listening in one of his monkish postures, hands joined, fingers against his lips. When the tape was finished, I complained about the brevity of the interview.

"I'd only a few minutes at the end to ask questions. Will it be like that with the others, too? I mean, will there always be such a limited time?"

"I'm afraid so, James," he said. "They all have other things on their minds than our investigation."

"Maybe I'll have a chance to talk to Anna again," I said. "I'd really like to."

Reeve Blair's grey eyes seemed stern to me now.

"Listen to me, James. Put Anna Grubach out of your mind. There's one thing you must understand, and you must always remind yourself of it. These people are as good as dead. They aren't much more than cadavers who can still talk. Never allow yourself to like them too much, or hate them too much. They may be interesting characters but they're no more substantial than those people you meet in your dreams." His voice became more gentle, more wheedling. "Please remember what I say, for your own good. Our trades are quite similar, and this is one of the things we have to learn very early. Otherwise we'd go mad."

I promised him I'd try to do as he said and he seemed satisfied. Now I brought up the topic of the reading material he'd delivered the night before.

"Did you know what was in the envelope Aiken sent?" I asked.

"Those pages about the Festival of the Mysterium? Yes, I read them over. You must have noticed how erratic the spelling was. In those days there weren't any rules. And I'm sure you're not aware of the history of that word 'mysterium,' James. It's quite fascinating."

He began talking earnestly about the origins of the word. As I listened, I couldn't help noticing that this odd policeman had the same kind of mind as some of the professors whose lectures had put me to sleep at university.

REEVE BLAIR'S BRIEF LECTURE ON A WORD

(transcribed verbatim from tape by me, James Maxwell)

"*Mysterium* is an old Latin word that derives from an even older Greek word. In the classical era, it referred almost exclusively to certain secret religious rites only initiates could attend; and that quasi-theological, quasi-supernatural sense of the word has survived to this today.

"But by the Middle Ages, we find it also being used for dramatic performances — the so-called mystery plays. And, coincidentally, in that same period, 'mystery' began to be used for any trade, or craft, or art. The various craft-guilds used the word freely, and in fact it was the guildsmen who were responsible for putting on the mystery plays. Apprentices, when they were indentured to a trade, swore to embrace its 'art or mystery' — that was the prescribed phrase. Each guild had its initiation secrets and its trade secrets which were protected by elaborate safeguards and rituals. Pharmacists and physicians in particular didn't want anyone else to know the formulae for their elixirs.

"Of course, James, you are aware that the study of language is not quite scientific. So it should not surprise you that not everyone agrees upon the origins of the word 'mystery.' One group of philologists says that 'mystery' used in reference to the trades comes not from *mysterium*, but from *ministerium*, meaning 'mastery' — a derivation which does have a certain common-sense appeal. But be that as it may, all scholars agree that 'mastery/mystery' and 'mystery/mastery' are words whose roots have now become so intertwined they're impossible to separate. Take, for instance, this Festival of the Mysterium you read about — the one that was held in Carrick. The guilds came here and the secret rites were enacted here. The drama they performed — the *Mysterium Mysteriorum* — was no doubt a tribute to both the crafts and their mysteries. It is possible even that the performers were chosen from the tradespeople of this town, and that Carrick itself, normally their workplace, became for one week the stage for their performance."

———————

Performance! When Reeve Blair used that word, I couldn't help thinking of how, just a few minutes before he arrived, I'd had that vague sense of being involved in a dramatic performance since I'd come to Carrick.

But mainly I marvelled at the Reeve's knowledge: he might have been a scholar as well as a monk.

"Why Aiken wanted you to read those pages, I'm not sure, James," he said. "He'll tell you that himself in due course. For now, we mustn't allow ourselves to be distracted by those references to punishments and apothecaries and potions, for perhaps that's all they are — distractions. The mysteries you and I have come here to Carrick to investigate are the mysteries associated with a great crime, and we can't permit anything to divert our attention from them."

"Just out of curiosity, though," I said, "what do those words on the title page mean — *certum quia impossibile?*"

"They're a short form of another Latin phrase — a paradox." I think, in spite of what he'd said earlier, he didn't mind this opportunity of showing his knowledge a little. "Loosely translated, they mean that something you always thought quite impossible may actually be the only solution to your problem. Worth remembering, in our profession."

He now drew a folder out of his brief-case. "I'm glad you enjoyed your reading, James. I've brought you some more. Today, Sentinel Hogg gave me these for you." He took a discoloured pamphlet and a page of old newspaper out of the folder.

"Have you read them yourself?" I asked. "Will they be of any use to me?"

"I've read them; but you must read them for yourself and draw your own conclusions. And remember, James: it's not always the clues that are right before your eyes that are significant. Some of the most important things in life can only be seen with peripheral vision. That's another one of the secrets of our trade."

When Reeve Blair was gone, I unfolded the page of newsprint. It was tanned with age; the date showed it had been published near the end of the War. I read it over carefully.

POW CAMPS   A SUCCESS

Camp Zero (for security reasons, I cannot give its exact location) lies several miles to the north-east of a remote village under the shadow of the hills, on a rugged plateau of moorland.

The morning I was there, I watched all fifteen of the prisoners of war making their short march along the moorland road past a pond that is popular with local fishermen. They were headed for the coal-mine only a few hundred yards away. The job the prisoners are here for is to fill the places of the men from the village who normally work at the mine during peacetime. These POWs wore the standard gear of khaki trousers and short jackets, hardly adequate for the chill morning air up here among the hills, and yet too warm for the temperatures they face daily underground.

It was fascinating to see the enemy this close up and not have to worry about them. Most of them had the standard black hair, and one of them had a black beard. One, however, had a shock of red hair, which surprised me — he looked just like one of our own. Some of them were of a stocky build, probably from a peasant class; two were noticeably bald. But they were all very young.

None of them appeared cowed by their situation; they walked upright and seemed quite cheerful. They marched at a steady pace under the scrutiny of a guard with a rifle.

I walked along behind, right to the mine itself. The POWs seemed to know the routine: they went into a shed for their safety-helmets, picks and shovels, then they marched over to the mine elevator, a hut with a sort of Ferris wheel on top of it. A local man in a miner's uniform took charge. He ordered the POWs into the cage. They filed in and grasped the leather roof straps. The cage door shut, the cable slammed into gear and down they went into the mine.

A few local men still work on the surface. One of them told me that when the POWs reach the bottom of the shaft, they climb into bogeys that carry them a mile to the coal face. When they arrive there, the prisoner who acts as foreman assigns some to work with picks. The others shovel coal into the bogeys that return to the surface. One or two spend all day putting up the roof-props in the tunnels and extending the electrical wiring as it is needed. They eat all their meals and perform all their physical needs underground. Smoking is absolutely forbidden. Each shift lasts from seven in the morning till four in the afternoon. Then they return to the surface and go back to camp.

The guard took me back to have a look at the empty camp. A mesh fence tipped with barbed wire surrounds the whole compound. Electric bulbs overhang the fence every few yards. A wooden guard tower with an "O" (for Zero) painted on it looks over the whole camp. Inside, there are five Nissen huts. They are painted green on the outside, for camouflage purposes, though the guard told me no enemy planes have ever been spotted in this area. Three of the huts are dormitories with pot-bellied stoves at the end facing the door. A fourth hut closes the square: a lavatory and shower-room occupy one half, a kitchen and mess-hall the other. The fifth hut, which stands apart on the south-west side is green too; but a white picket fence surrounds it. This is the residence of the camp commandant and the guards.

My guide was full of information. He said that in addition to their work in the mine, the POWs perform one other civic task. On a specific day each week they are taken to the village. For the entire morning their job is to get rid of garbage, sweep the streets, wash windows, mow the Green and assist villagers with gardening. At lunchtime, the POWs are allocated to various families around the village for their meal, three to each household.

The guard said the POWs appreciate the feeling of going into a warm house, and washing their hands, and sitting down at a table with a table-cloth to eat a decent meal. They told him they can almost believe that they are in their own country, doing the domestic rituals of free men.

I must add here that when I later spoke to the village women, they admitted they enjoyed the experience too. Those whose men were abroad said it allowed them to make a special occasion of the day and show the enemy the traditional Island hospitality. Of course, not all the villagers co-operate. Some families apparently will have nothing to do with the prisoners.

The guard said the POWs were surprisingly docile, and there had been no real problems. Only three guards were needed each day: one (himself) to take the men to and from the mine; and two to share the watch-tower duty at night. An officer from Stroven served as part-time commandant. I asked the guard what he thought of this way of employing captured soldiers. He said, so far as Carrick was concerned, the experiment was "a great success."

The author of the article was not named. Alongside it was a photograph, and under that a caption: "Prisoners at Camp Zero." Two rows of men were facing the camera; those in front were seated on benches, those behind were standing. They looked as innocent as a football team.

The faces of the prisoners were hard to make out in the pointillised newsprint, so I tried holding the paper at arm's length. Dots blended together into tunics, baggy pants and work boots; but the faces became more distant and just as anonymous. I couldn't match any of the men in the picture with the descriptions, though one man in the middle of the back row did seem to have a beard.

I turned my attention to the pamphlet; it was only six

pages long. Its title was *The Upland Rifles: The Incident at the Mord River Bridge*, by (the late) Colonel W.W. Morton. It was part of a War Series and was stamped CARRICK LIBRARY — REFERENCE ONLY. The cover was plain white, and the tops of the pages were badly stained. I caught the faint whiff of a now familiar smell. I put my nose to the pages, but it wasn't there. I sniffed at my left hand, the one Anna had touched. Yes, there it was. I had brought the smell with me. I brushed the fingers of my right hand through my hair, and found it there too; I could even smell it on my sweater.

I stood up, carefully took off my clothes and hung them on a hook on the outside of the closet door. I went into the shower and stood under the hot water for a long time, scrubbing myself. Then I dried off, put on my pyjamas and sat on the wooden chair. Uncontaminated, I picked up the pamphlet and began reading.

That winter had been an especially cold one all over the Continent. On the last day of March, in a sunless dawn, we marshalled in the city square and prepared to advance. At precisely eight o'clock, on a signal given, the Third Army left the ruins of the cathedral and the town hall behind us, and marched through bombed-out suburbs for an hour before reaching the countryside.

Our advance to the banks of the swollen Mord River lasted for six hours without a break. When we reached the embankment road, our men were silent, gazing the half-mile across the river at the hills and forests of the enemy's heartland. For year after devastating year we had suffered hunger and thirst, we had seen friends and comrades dead or wounded, we had fought pitched battles, escaped death in innumerable ambushes and strafings and skirmishes; now, it was our turn to make the final, triumphal onslaught.

At three o'clock we arrived at the Mord River Bridge.

We ate a hot stew while the Engineer Corps checked the bridge's structure for explosives. All of us, officers as well as ranks, joked while we ate. We even complimented the cooks, a rare thing up till then. We could not help our feeling of jubilation. The War would soon be over, and we would be on our way home to the Island at long last.

At three-thirty, precisely, word came back that the bridge was safe and the Third began to cross.

Everything went smoothly. Four armoured vehicles of the Upland Rifles entered the bridge. After them, as usual, came the regimental band playing the pibroch "The Men of the North." Now followed the Ninth Battalion, composed mainly of men from the hill districts, with a long tradition as fighters. Interspersed with the ranks were trucks laden with supplies.

My Company would normally have been among the first to cross, but we were ordered to remain on the south side, a hundred yards down river, with the anti-aircraft guns. We were to guard against any unwelcome surprises from the skies during the crossing.

As it happened, we were perfectly positioned to witness the disaster.

Inside minutes, the bridge was a mass of marching men and heavily loaded vehicles. We became aware that the centre span, which was about two hundred yards wide, was starting to sway, slowly at first, in a harmless sort of way, as though it were swinging to the music of the pipes. I don't think those on the bridge even noticed. Then, all of a sudden, the entire span twisted like a huge snake. The cables the bridge hung from began to snap, producing dreadful chords that rang in our ears as we stood horrified. Trucks and men began to spill higgledy-piggledy, in slow motion, a hundred feet into the swollen winter river.

We could do nothing but watch. Some of the soldiers were lucky: a few at the rear of the column managed to scramble back onto the firm part of the bridge. The others realized what was happening, but had no hope; they were swept downward by the accumulated weight of their comrades behind them and the heavy trucks. Several men managed to hold on to the girders, and swung for a while till their arms weakened and they plunged to their deaths.

One or two, incredibly, survived the fall into the river, and resurfaced in the icy current in spite of their heavy clothing and packs full of ammunition. Our commander gave orders to us to spread out and pull out those who made it to the bank. No one did make it.

We watched all these things with horror and yet with relief that we ourselves had been spared.

Later, the Major in charge of the Engineers who had inspected the Mord River Bridge claimed the enemy must have sawn part-way through the cables. But some of his men said they had warned him this kind of bridge was not built to hold masses of men marching in unison; that the rhythmic movement would cause structural failure. They said our display of triumph was the problem: we had slaughtered ourselves.

A sadder note: one platoon consisting solely of men from Carrick was on the central span when it collapsed. It has always been a tradition in the Upland Rifles, for the sake of morale, to keep men from the same area together. So, on that day, in that freezing river, nineteen men from Carrick died: a disaster of incredible magnitude for such a small town.

Such is the toll war exacts of us.

Patterns! Even I could see the patterns as I thought about what I'd just read. So Carrick's population had been decimated once before — only a generation ago! And I was sure there must be some connection between the prisoners of war at Camp Zero (the red-painted circles! Anna's reference to "the prisoners"!) and this incident long ago at the Mord River Bridge. All of this must be related in some way to these other things that had happened recently in Carrick.

I felt quite exhilarated. I realized I was only an apprentice in such matters, but I was sure that in time

I would understand everything — I would see the entire picture emerge from its negative, colours and all. Nevertheless, I should be patient. Reeve Blair after all had read the same material and he surely saw the significance of it. Why hadn't he said something? I remembered the advice he'd given me on my first day at Carrick.

"When we approach great mysteries," he'd said, "we are like men who set out to climb mountains; we need to look them over carefully first from a distance, to gain a perspective, or we may take the impossible route."

With that in mind, I calmed myself. I put away the papers, switched off the light and climbed into the hard bed. The wind had been noticeable for quite a while, and seemed even stronger now. It howled, scratched, shook the hut, groping for any crack to get in by.

I was warm and sleepy and didn't wish to think any more. So it was, thinking about not thinking, that I did eventually stop thinking and abandoned myself to a howling wind and the image of a beautiful face with green eyes.

The next day, my third day at Carrick, I woke at seven-thirty and lay for a while remembering a dream in which I'd walked down an endless street of some town I'd never been in before. The faces of the people, of the children playing, were each distinct and unique. Who are these dream-people? I wondered. Where do they come from? Where do they go after we wake?

After toast and coffee in the mess-hall, I walked down to the town around nine for my next appointment. The morning was dry, and the wind was only a breeze, but the necks of the hills had high collars of rain around them, and there was a red tint in the eastern sky, as though blood were seeping through. As I walked, I wondered what it would be like to live permanently in a place like Carrick, if city people would be strong enough for it. Those who spend all their lives in such places must bear some watching, I thought.

A caped figure was coming towards me on the road from Carrick. It was Anna's nurse and she looked tired.

"Good-morning," I said. "How is she?"

"Died an hour ago," she said abruptly. Then she must have noticed how shocked I was, for she stopped and spoke more kindly, perhaps remembering I wasn't used to what was going on here.

"She didn't suffer at all. She just talked and talked. She used words I didn't recognize, like some foreign language. She laughed a lot too, then she turned her face to the wall and curled up like a baby. And that was that."

I walked on slowly down towards Carrick. All I could think of was that I wouldn't see Anna Grubach again, and that I really had liked her. I was quite unprepared for the grief I felt. I remembered Reeve Blair's advice to treat Anna and the others as though they were no more substantial than dream-people — just like those I'd met last night. I tried to think of her that way but it wasn't the same.

When I came into the village, I saw the military ambulance drawn up outside her store and soldiers going in and out. I didn't have the stomach to go past, so I took the path across the Green. I thought I saw a figure at the upper window of the Pharmacy, but I pretended not to notice and kept my eyes on the path. Fragments of red glass glittered up at me.

The Keep was my destination that morning; sad or not, I told myself I must concentrate on the business at hand. The building itself was old, built of granite and square shaped. It looked even more angular against the background of smooth, rounded hills. Like some of the other impressive buildings here, it was massive for such a small town. Reeve Blair said it looked big enough to hold everyone in Carrick.

I put Anna out of my head and climbed the three wide steps. The soldier on guard looked me over suspiciously then swung his rifle to one side. I opened the heavy door and went in.

The floor of the reception area was of flagstones; on one side there was a high wooden desk in front of two rows of wooden benches that might have come from a church. At the far side, a tiny coal fire burned in a huge hearth. A nurse with close-cropped grey hair was sitting on a stool near the fireplace. When she saw me, she got up and told me to follow her.

"He's in the lock-up. It saves us going up and down stairs to his rooms. You'd better wear these." She handed me a pair of industrial ear protectors, just as Reeve Blair had said she would.

I followed her through a doorway that opened onto a row of cells. The usual sour smell of an institution greeted us — and one other smell, familiar to me now, and so strong in here it seemed capable of seeping through the pores. The nurse pointed to the cell at the end of the row.

"One hour. No more." Then she went back through the door to the reception area. I switched on my tape-recorder, and walked slowly along the short passage way.

Through the open door of his cell I saw Sentinel Hogg lying propped up on a bunk, alone. Even under the blankets, there was no mistaking the big body, the short neck. A caged bulb illuminated walls of brown that were textured as though the colour had been smeared on, not brushed; the window would have been big enough for a head to go through, but for three bars over the opening. A washbasin and a toilet took up part of one wall; Sentinel Hogg's bunk filled most of the other, along with a wooden chair. Lying on the chipped tiles of the floor was a sheaf of typed paper — it looked like another copy of Aiken's narrative.

The Sentinel was preoccupied rubbing his jaw slowly with his fingers till he noticed me by the door.

"You must be Maxwell!"

I quickly put on the ear protectors, for his voice was like a blow to the head. It had been amplified in some way by the poison, so that it was as good as a weapon; but he himself looked quite friendly. His eyes were green, and I noticed, were unflickering. He stretched his right hand out to me. It was a small, fine hand, as delicate as a tentacle from that huge body. His hand in mine was moist, but cold. I remembered Anna's warm hand; he may have read my mind, for he said, or roared:

"Poor Anna. She died this morning, you know."

I sat on the wooden chair and loosened my collar; I could endure the noise of his voice, but the smell when he stirred among the blankets was overwhelming.

"I've known her since she was an infant," he said. I thought he was going to talk more about her, but he abruptly changed the subject. "Enough about Anna. Did that Reeve from the South give you those things to read last night?"

"Yes."

"Good. There are some other pieces of information I've been instructed to pass on to you."

Then he began to tell me (and the whole world!) what he knew. I'd had the impression from Aiken's narrative that the Sentinel was not a talkative man, so I was surprised at how forthcoming he was. He licked his lips incessantly as though he found the words sweet to the taste. His tongue sprayed me as he talked and he frequently caressed his jaw the way a fly massages itself.

"Can you imagine, Maxwell, what it was like for me long ago, during the early days of the War?"

THE TESTIMONY OF SENTINEL HOGG

(transcribed from tape by me, James Maxwell)

His three brothers and his father were all fishermen in Malla, a village on the north-west coast of the Island. It was hard enough for them to make a living from the sea in peacetime; it was impossible when enemy ships were cruising the fishing grounds. He was the youngest and they decided he should leave the village and find himself some other profession.

He was the right size to be a policeman, so he signed up for two years' training at the Academy in the Capital. While he was there, he saw his share of air raids and bombed-out buildings. He saw more than his share of worse horrors — the ruined bodies, the cratered minds. His training ended just before the War did; a vacancy arose in Carrick, he applied for it, and was delighted to be posted there.

Carrick, when he arrived, was mainly a town of women waiting for the end of the War and the return of their men, only a few of whom had been exempted from the armed forces: the professionals such as Doctor Rankin and Alexander Aiken, the elderly such as Jakob Grubach. Some experienced miners were spared, too, so that they could supervise the prisoners of war who worked the mine that supplied coal for the fireplaces of Carrick.

THE DEATHS OF SO MANY Carrick men at the Mord River Bridge was the cause of grief such as Sentinel Hogg had never seen before.

But around that same time, another disaster occurred. Not abroad, on the battle-front, but in Carrick itself.

Late on a Friday morning in March Sentinel Hogg was standing at the high desk filling out his weekly report. He was hungry and beginning to anticipate the lunch special at the cafe. He had just started to clear his desk when he heard, for the first time since he'd arrived in Carrick, the whine of the siren from the Mine. That startled him, for in wartime, the siren was only to be used as an air-raid warning.

He ran out into the street and looked up. Other towns-people were already outside too, all of them looking up at the grey sky. They could see no planes and hear no drone of engines; but still the siren wailed on. Miss Balfour was the first to notice the pall of black smoke rising over the Cairn. Sentinel Hogg understood then that something awful must have happened at the Mine.

The old fire truck was brought out of its shed and dusted off. Sentinel Hogg and the women of the Volunteer Fire Brigade climbed in and set off for the Mine.

It took twenty minutes for them to get there. When they arrived and shut off the engine, the Sentinel heard no howling of the siren. The mine foreman and two guards from the camp were standing beside the shaft. A tangle of cables hung limply from the big wheel, and there was no longer any smoke.

"It was an explosion down there," the foreman told the Sentinel. "The cables are broken away from the cage, and there's no way down. We can't do anything. I've phoned for a rescue crew from the Capital." This foreman, a tall young man with the white hair and white eyelashes of an albino, was very upset.

Accustomed as he was to city disasters, the Sentinel found this situation strange. The only signs of anything extraordinary were those dangling cables. For the rest, nature was the same as ever — the occasional screech of a whaup in the distance, the occasional sighing of the light wind, and otherwise silence. The human beings stood around shouting now and then down the shaft, but hearing only the echoes of their own voices.

Other townspeople, mainly women, arrived in cars or

on foot all that afternoon. Many of them had noticed, as they passed the St Giles Pond, that the water was very low. Some of them speculated that perhaps it had burst through the layer of rock into the Mine and flooded the galleries that were known to run under the pond.

Dusk came, and the Sentinel and the townspeople could do nothing else but go back down to Carrick. The two guards stayed by the elevator, just in case. The night turned bitterly cold, with a dusting of snow.

The rescue crew didn't arrive from the Capital till Saturday afternoon. A series of desperate air raids on the shipyards for three consecutive nights had kept them busy, and they were tired. Their chief confessed to the Sentinel that this accident at Carrick involving a group of enemy prisoners was not at the top of their list of priorities.

A crowd of townspeople, including the Sentinel, watched as two of the crew were lowered by ropes down the shaft as near as they could to the galleries at the bottom which were indeed flooded. The two crewmen could see no floating bodies and they could hear no sounds but the lapping of water. When they were hauled back up to the surface, the two men said they thought they had smelt gas. They speculated that a flash explosion of underground gases had cracked the membrane of rock between the mine and the St Giles Pond, and caused the inundation.

It was dusk again and everyone went back to Carrick. The men of the rescue crew spent that night at The Stag. Even though it was wartime, there was no shortage of whisky for them.

A few days later, a Commission of Inquiry came to Carrick and made some cursory inquiries. The commissioners endorsed the findings of the rescue crew, and ordered that the Mine be boarded up and Camp Zero dismantled.

After that, it was rare for the townspeople even to mention the matter. Though no one said it outright, the Sentinel understood that as far as Carrick was concerned, the deaths of the POWs helped make up, at least in some measure, for the deaths of the Carrick men at the Mord River Bridge.

FROM THE POINT OF VIEW of Sentinel Hogg, that was that. Carrick became home to him. The next year, he married the widow of one of the men who'd died at the Mord River Bridge, and she looked after him well for twenty years, till she herself died. He looked forward to retirement among his friends in the town he had served. All was well.

Until this recent vandalism began. That first incident — the mutilation of the Monument — left a bad taste in his mouth. He was quite capable of dealing with the occasional fight outside The Stag at closing time, or of investigating the occasional case of incest. He had lots of practice in such matters. But the vandalism outraged him and made no sense to him. He felt out of his depth.

"Kirk's the man. Watch the Colonial, Kirk." So Aiken had said, from the start.

The Sentinel knew about Martin Kirk, how he spent most of his days at work in the hills and, after a while, most of his evenings with Anna Grubach. The Sentinel

had met him several times and found him to be a
pleasant enough man, with disconcerting blue eyes,
a man who asked disconcerting questions.

"Did you ever visit a fortune-teller, Sentinel Hogg?"
Kirk asked him one day on the Green during a conversation about the now defunct Carrick Festival.

"No, I never did," said the Sentinel.

"You're not a Carrick man by birth?"

The Sentinel again said, no; he was from a fishing village in the north of the Island. Kirk then said he too had
spent time in a fishing village — but it was in a tropical
country, far away. "As a matter of fact, Sentinel, I
attended a kind of festival there," he said.

THE FESTIVAL OF SAN ISIDORO was cele-
brated annually in the fishing village named after the
saint, a place of low buildings, peeling paint, ragged
vultures, mosquitoes and the smell of human waste. Kirk
took a room in the damp hotel for the weekend.

On the first day of the festival, the morning, like
most mornings there, was hot and humid. Kirk joined
the crowd gathered in the *zocala* to watch the ritual
firing of an old cannon by some villagers dressed as con-
quistadores: they aimed the cannon out to sea (perhaps
to wake up the saint, perhaps to attract the fish),
primed it, and fired.

But the cannon was now too old even for such placid
games. The barrel exploded and pieces of it went flying
all over the place. No one seemed to be hurt, and the
crowd was ready to laugh; they didn't notice at first that
one young Indian (he and his wife had come in from

their jungle village for the festivities) holding his belly. A shard of the metal had ripped through his trousers and his bowels, nestling so far inside him that its sharp end was actually sticking out of his back just above the belt line.

Slowly he fell, his blood darkening the red soil of the square. He must have known he was as good as dead and he didn't want to die with that thing in him. Staring down at himself, he began probing with his right hand inside his ruined body pulling his intestines out of the way, that hand in there right up to the wrist, trying to get a grip on the metal. The crowd gathered round to watch. His wife, who had been standing beside him when the metal struck, implored him to stop, but he paid no attention to her. The local priest arrived on the scene to give the last rites and he snatched the dying man's arm away, scolding him as though he were a child in church, with his hand in his pocket. But the Indian kept putting it back in, and died with his hand in there, trying to grasp the pain.

His wife, who had been kneeling beside him, was inconsolable. It seems a fortune-teller had just told the couple they'd live long and have many children.

SENTINEL HOGG WAS MOVED by Kirk's story. He remembered shrapnel wounds he had seen when he worked in the Capital.

"Very sad," he said.

"Sad, yes. But did you know, Sentinel" (Kirk said this on the Green that day), "we're all supposed to be capable of telling the fortune of one other person in the world? The problem is knowing which person it is. Perhaps someone in Carrick can tell mine. Perhaps it's Robert Aiken. Or perhaps I can tell his."

ROBERT HAD BEEN DEEPLY suspicious of Kirk since the mutilation of the Monument, and had said so. But Sentinel Hogg couldn't believe it. Why, he wondered, would any man who talked as well as Kirk need to commit such an act?

Aiken shook his head.

"You're too impressed by words, Sentinel. You must get him away from Carrick," he said. "I don't trust him."

Lack of trust seemed to the Sentinel a flimsy basis for action. Nonetheless, after the vandalism at the graveyard, he phoned the Capital and asked for information on Kirk. And one morning after Kirk had left for the hills, he searched his hotel room. Aside from fishing tackle and clothing, he found notebooks full of illegible scribblings, little bottles of assorted powders, test tubes, and other odds and ends of what he took to be the tools of the hydrologist's trade. There was no axe, no spray-paint, nothing incriminating — nothing whatsoever.

THE DAY OF SWAINSTON'S MURDER was an awful day for Sentinel Hogg. He knew everything was completely out of his control now, he was as much a spectator as the others. When they brought the body down from the cottage and laid it in one of the cells, the warm air caused the dead man to expel gas loudly like a dead sheep, and the smell was awful. Robert said the body would decompose quickly if they didn't cover it in ice, so they heaped ice all over it.

The Sentinel phoned headquarters in the Capital, then went over to The Stag.

"He's in his room," Mitchell said, knowing why he'd come.

The Sentinel marched heavily up the stairs. He took a breath or two, then knocked at Kirk's door. Kirk did not look surprised to see him.

"I don't want to come in," said the Sentinel, awkwardly. "Stay in the hotel tomorrow till the detectives talk to you. All right?"

He didn't like the way those blue eyes looked at him, as though they were able to see that thing in a man he could never admit, even to himself.

ALONE IN THE KEEP the Sentinel found it hard to concentrate with Swainston's body next door. He hadn't slept well the night before (Miss Balfour had told him she'd slept badly too). He did what he rarely did on a working day: he poured himself a glass of Scotch and drank it down quickly. Then he sat by the fire and opened his mail. One letter was from Headquarters.

Sent Hogg:

Re: your inquiries about the Colonial, Martin Kirk. Our department has checked the subject with Immigration and Foreign Relations. Kirk is a certified hydrologist on a research project jointly supported by the Island and the Colony. He has no criminal record. Let us know if any further information is required.

Yours, etc.

He phoned Robert right away and read him the letter. "It doesn't matter now," Robert said.

Sentinel Hogg told him he'd confined Kirk to The Stag and that the detectives from the Capital would interrogate him when they arrived.

"I told you," Robert said, "it doesn't make any difference now."

DID IT MAKE ANY difference? Sentinel Hogg wondered. A few days later, Kirk was dead. And not long after that, the people of Carrick began dying, including the Sentinel himself. He didn't mind. He believed that if he had to die, Carrick wasn't such a bad place to die in.

———◆◆◆———

"No, Maxwell. It really isn't such a bad place to die in, is it?"

Sentinel Hogg didn't expect an answer from me. Anyway, I wasn't quite sure what he'd asked. I was glad I had the tape-recorder, for at times the ear protectors were inadequate and whatever he said was just an incomprehensible rumbling in my ears. Now he wiped his lips with his pyjama sleeve and pointed a delicate forefinger at the cell floor:

"It was in this very cell we laid Swainston's body."

He was talking now with a slight lisp. Though his voice was as loud as ever, his tongue was resting on his lower lip as though it were tired and he was rubbing his jaw furiously. For the first time, I noticed his eyelashes flickering a little, in the way Aiken had described.

My hour was almost up, so I asked him the question that had been on my mind.

"About the accident at the Mine," I said. "Was it really an accident, or was it deliberate?"

He didn't answer so I asked again, straight out:

"Was it an accident, or was it revenge for the deaths of the Carrick men at the Mord River Bridge?"

His face creased and he began laughing with his tongue protruding — the laugh of a plump gargoyle. He choked out:

"Ah! Good man, Maxwell!" He tried to control himself. "Those commissioners ruled it an accident, and how could I disagree with them? I'm only a simple policeman." He was having great difficulty with his tongue and the laughter. "Talk to Miss Balfour about it. She has things to tell you that you'll find very interesting."

His words were garbled and he was rubbing his jaw gingerly, as though all this talking really had damaged it.

"But I was hoping you'd help me find out the truth," I said. I shouldn't have said that, for his eyes filled with tears and he laughed so hard I thought he'd choke.

"Telling truth . . . is only possible . . . if you don't . . . know very much." That was exactly Anna's answer. He gasped it out, the rapid blinking of his eyelashes spraying tears around like a miniature garden sprinkler.

I waited till he'd composed his face again.

135

"You interrogated Kirk after Swainston's death along with those other police agents. What did he say?"

"Not a word. We questioned him about the vandalism and about the death of Swainston. We couldn't get a word out of him. That's why he was called to headquarters in the Capital. They have professional interrogators there."

He told me this, but he didn't seem interested any more. He pointed one tapered finger at Aiken's narrative lying on the floor. I could have guessed what he was going to ask.

"How did you like his portrayal of me?" He was looking at me anxiously. He seemed so jovial lying there, and so vulnerable in spite of his size, what could I say?

"It was certainly interesting," I said.

He sighed and smiled contentedly; he was nodding his head at almost the same speed as his flickering eyelids.

"You're right. No man can ask for more than that, can he?"

Just then I felt a hand on my shoulder. The nurse, wearing ear protectors, had come in and was saying something I couldn't hear.

"She says time's up," the Sentinel roared.

"Just let me ask you this before I go, Sentinel Hogg. How was Kirk involved? Why did Robert Aiken poison everyone, even his friends?"

"He got us all in the end, you're right about that." The Sentinel was smiling at the idea, as though it were admirable and not monstrous.

"But why?" I myself was shouting now as though he

136

had a hearing problem. "Anna said if I asked you, you'd tell me about motives."

"Think about this, Maxwell." He had a sly look about him. "Sometimes the motive has to be invented to accommodate the crime. Got it? That's all I can say. You just keep doing what you're doing, and you'll be fine."

I wanted an explanation of that, but he roared: "That's it. I've said all I was supposed to. Thank you, young Maxwell, for listening. Can you imagine having to tell any of this to that Reeve from the South?"

I stood outside the Keep with my ears ringing. Gradually I noticed other sounds again: the wind had become strong enough to make the pines on the Green jostle against each other. I took a deep breath. The humped book-ends of hills on each side of Carrick were stark and clear. I opened my coat and let the astringent wind scour away the acrid smell from my clothes.

Reeve Blair came walking towards me from the direction of the Monument, his hands clasped behind his back in one of his meditating postures.

"Well?" he asked when he saw me.

"Noisy," I said.

The Reeve nodded. "He reminds me of a town crier I sat beside at one of those official banquets. It's hard to have an intimate conversation with a town crier."

"But he did tell me some things that are quite incredible," I said. "These people have a tradition of mass exterminations! I only knew about the poisoning of the towns-people and the deaths of the Carrick men at the Mord

River Bridge. I thought that was bad enough. But now Sentinel Hogg has as much as admitted that the prisoners of war at Camp Zero were murdered. Did you know that?"

"I've heard the rumours, yes," he said. "You can let me hear the tape tonight. You'd better be on your way to your next appointment." He was assessing me. "Will you be all right, James?"

"Thanks, I'm fine. I'm following your advice." And indeed I was trying, without much success, to make myself think of Sentinel Hogg as nothing but a phantasm with a loud voice. My words had the right casual ring to them, but I was happy to get away from those astute grey eyes.

Miss Balfour's rooms were above the Library but quite separate from it. The only access to them was from an alleyway that ran between the Library and the Church. A soldier was on guard at the bottom of a set of iron stairs. At first he looked quite alarmed when he saw me, then he relaxed.

"One hour," he said.

As I climbed the stairs, they gonged like a xylophone ascending the scale, and chimed out the high note when I reached the landing. Before the sound had faded, I heard a voice.

"Kim oon!"

This odd greeting came to me through the green painted door that was slightly ajar. Shreds of a familiar smell also seeped from behind it, to be snatched by the wind and carried off to the south.

I braced myself, pushed the door open and went inside. Miss Balfour, the Carrick librarian, lay in her bed in a room with just enough room left for a table and a stuffed armchair. Books were piled on the table, on both window sills, on ledges, on every surface that would hold them, including the floor; I had to weave my way between pyramids of books. A copy of Aiken's narrative was lying on the armchair. The room was very cold: the fire looked as though it hadn't been lit for a long time. As I switched on my tape-recorder, I made to close the door.

"Dun't shoat it," she said. "The cheel kips me from fulling aslop. I dun't weesh to gae to slop yat."

Reeve Blair had told me how the poison had given Miss Balfour this unique dialect. He said it sounded all the odder, coming from one who had once been such a pedant in her use of words.

She was propped up on the bed, just like the others. Under wispy, grey hair, her face was so transparent it was easy to see the labyrinth of veins. The collar of her white nightgown half-covered the bulge of a goitre; a brown mole as big as a nipple stood out in the middle of the bulge.

Her eyes were remarkable. They were clear and blue, unusual in a country with so little sun; they were light blue, like watering holes in a wilderness.

"Sue yo're Mexwill. Oh'm glod ta moot ye. Wa ell heave ir lottle bats ond pisses ta toll ye."

I sat down in the armchair near the bed while she talked in that parody of a language. But I didn't find it too hard to understand her for she spoke slowly; her lips were anaesthetized by the cold of that room, perhaps, and the words could only squeeze through them with difficulty.

"Ees ut stronge ta veesut Cerrick? Ameeng sa muny dode und deeing?" These questions didn't require answers from me; as if their purpose were simply to test my tape-recorder and make sure it was in working order — no more than that.

"Noo, sartin thongs oh moost toll ya. Whon ee wis a yang wowman, ell ir tribbles sterted."

Watching her, it was easy to believe that her grotesqueness might have been beauty, once. I was torn between marvelling at the transformation in her, and wishing she would let me close the door. In that cold, cold room she began telling of the day the prisoners of war arrived in Carrick.

"Cun ye imogine whit it was leek ta soo the inimy for the feerst toom?"

THE TESTIMONY OF
MISS BALFOUR

(transcribed from tape into intelligible language and compressed by me, James Maxwell)

She closed the library and went down to join the others on the Green. It was a sunny, cold day. She felt it was rather uncouth to stand there gawping, but she couldn't restrain her curiosity.

She heard the rumbling then saw the army truck come rolling into the Green and trundle past. Its tarpaulin cover was wide open at the back. The prisoners, dark-haired men for the most part, were manacled to benches; they looked out at the women, and some of them smiled in a cautious way. One, a handsome man with a beard, seated right at the back, looked directly at Miss Balfour for a long moment. She did not allow herself to smile. This was the enemy, she told herself. This was the enemy.

But in the days and months that followed their arrival, she, like the other townspeople, came to appreciate the prisoners' work at the Mine, for it meant cheap coal again. And on Saturdays it was good to see them cleaning the streets of Carrick, repairing potholes, tidying up the Green and painting doors. On occasion they polished the floor of the Library. In the summer, they mowed lawns too, and tended neglected gardens.

These activities, all the townspeople welcomed; but not the policy of inviting prisoners to dinner in the homes of Carrick. Some of those whose husbands were fighting at the front were offended; they argued that the practice was nothing short of treasonous. How could they tell their husbands in their weekly letters that they'd had their foes over for Sunday dinner? But other townspeople saw no harm in it: the War was ended for these prisoners, they said; these men were the enemy no longer.

Miss Balfour remained neutral.

SHE WAS LOOKING OUT of the Library window on a wet Saturday afternoon almost a year after the prisoners arrived; she saw Alexander Aiken come out of the Pharmacy stealthily, cross the Green, and get into his car. She wondered why it was parked so far from the Pharmacy on such a day. She saw him slump over the steering wheel, his head on his arms. She knew better than to go out and ask him what was wrong. She admired him, this quiet man who had been exempted from military service because of his profession and his delicate health. He had recently married a woman from the Capital.

Though Miss Balfour did not go outside that day and ask Alexander what was wrong, she did ask him months later — when he was ready for questions and was willing to give answers. She asked, and he told her what happened.

On that Saturday when all his tribulations began, he, Alexander Aiken, had diverged from his usual ritual. In the morning, he had done what he always did. He had revved up his old Mercedes and driven to the various pharmacies around the hills, delivering his home-made elixirs (he was an amateur herbalist) and picking up supplies of pharmaceuticals. Around noon, as usual, he had reached Stroven to have lunch at The Chieftain with Sanders, a local pharmacist who had been a friend since their university days. Normally, they would sit for hours discussing the latest developments in herbal medicine, their shared hobby. Normally, at around three o'clock, Alexander would drive back to Carrick to be home for dinner.

But on this particular Saturday, this awful Saturday, things went wrong. When Alexander reached Stroven, Sanders was waiting for him at the door of The Chieftain to say he would have to forgo lunch —

he had to go to the Capital on a business matter. Alexander did not mind too much. After all, how nice it would be, he thought, to go home to Carrick early, and spend the afternoon with his wife, who was expecting their first child. How pleased she would be, he thought.

He drove home through the northern pass, delighting as always in the high moorlands, the blunt hills, the occasional glimpse of a deer or a hare. A heavy rain began to fall so he had to be extra cautious on that winding, narrow road. He noticed, as he rounded one corner, a large crow perched on a stone dyke that bordered the road. He saw another one after that, too, on a gate post. Perched there, in the rain, motionless.

He reached Carrick about one o'clock and passed a squad of prisoners from Camp Zero; they were wearing long, green slickers and were spreading gravel on the shoulder of the road where it entered the town. He cruised into Carrick. Instead of parking the Mercedes outside the Pharmacy, he drove to the far side of the Green and parked behind the pines. He wanted his early return to be a surprise to his wife.

He got out of the car and slinked round the perimeter of the Green, keeping his hat down over his eyes, hugging the walls of the buildings till he reached the Pharmacy. The CLOSED sign was in the door, just as he had left it. He turned his key gently in the lock and eased himself inside, closing the door softly behind him. He unlaced his wet shoes and left them on the mat. Then he tiptoed to the back of the store and began to climb to his rooms.

The wooden stairs were warped with age, but he was not heavy and had learnt since boyhood how to distribute his weight over the uneven boards, how to brace his toes in the corners to prevent creaking. He couldn't help smiling at the thought of how surprised his wife would be. He was smiling because he loved her, even more deeply now that she was to have his child. It made his eyes moist just to think of that.

He heard her voice just as he reached the last few stairs; but it was a sound he had never heard from her before — she was moaning loudly, obviously in pain.

In that instant of terror, the image of her lying on the floor in a pool of blood, miscarrying their baby in solitude, jolted his very being and he was able to spring up the remaining stairs like the athlete he had never been. He heard, even in mid-spring, the other, deeper voice.

Alexander stopped silently at the top of the stairs. Clothes were lying around on the living-room floor: here, a green slicker glistening, socks with patched heels, grey trousers, muddy boots; there, a slight blue dress (his favourite), her stockings, her crumpled white underclothes.

The deep voice was moaning now in harmony with his wife's moans. Alexander crept towards the open bedroom door and saw, reflected in the dresser mirror, the pale flesh of intertwined bodies, the long, fair hair of the one, the black hair, the black beard of the other.

Alexander Aiken retreated down the stairs, an empty man, feather light. He floated across the wet street, across the Green. He climbed into his car, shut the door, sunk his head onto the wheel, and he wept.

After a while he collected himself, thankful no one had seen him cross the Green, thankful for the misted car. He opened the window a crack and kept watch through the pines. A half-hour passed and the door of the Pharmacy opened. The bearded man in his slicker squinted up and down the street, stepped out, pulled the door shut and walked briskly westward in the direction of the party of prisoners who had been working on the road. Alexander watched till he disappeared from sight.

Miss Balfour, from the Library window, had seen it all: Alexander sitting in his car; the prisoner leaving the Pharmacy. She, who knew what must have happened, did not go to Alexander that day. She waited and waited, month after month, till Alexander Aiken confided in her. That was after other, more public disasters struck the town: the deaths of the Carrick men at the Mord River Bridge and the drowning of the prisoners at the Mine.

THE MORNING THE SIREN at the Mine began its howl, Miss Balfour was the first to notice the smoke's exclamation point over the Cairn, and she was among the first to follow the fire brigade truck. She made that journey in the front passenger seat of Alexander Aiken's Mercedes — she felt unwelcome. Alexander himself was driving, Doctor Rankin and Jakob Grubach sat in the back. She saw how Alexander's hands trembled as he drove.

"I wonder what's happened," she said. None of the three men responded. She looked at Alexander, then at the two behind her. They avoided looking at her. Aiken drove quite fast, but slowed the car a little as they passed the St Giles Pond. They could see its level had dropped by at least twenty feet, exposing to the air a great fleshy ring of underwater vegetation.

In a few seconds more they reached the Mine, and they knew from the way Sentinel Hogg greeted them that there was nothing to be done.

"A terrible accident," he said.

The mine foreman had a different point of view.

"It was no accident," he mumbled to Miss Balfour. "There are some here know that."

She paid no heed to him. She had been watching Alexander. He had walked right past Sentinel Hogg and looked down into the shaft. She had heard him ask one of the soldiers: "Are they all dead?"

The soldier said he thought they must be.

"Was no one spared?" Alexander asked. "Absolutely no one?"

The soldier said no, no one was spared. At that point, Miss Balfour saw Doctor Rankin come and take Alexander by the arm and lead him to the verge of the gravel road. And there Alexander sat down and put his head in his hands in a way she had seen before. His shoulders convulsed and she thought he must be weeping; but when she went to console him, he looked up and his eyes were quite dry.

THE WAR ENDED and Alexander's wife gave birth to a son, Robert. She herself died a month later. Miss Balfour did all a woman could to comfort Alexander. She spent more and more time in the rooms above the Pharmacy, helping him bring up his child. In Alexander's face she could already see the first rough sketches of his illness. It was she who had to tell him, when his son was in the spring of his fifth year:

"It's time you took Robert to the taming."

"I can't," said Alexander. So she herself took the boy.

A TAMING PEN had been set up on the Green, and townspeople who kept collies for pets brought the pups there. They were such fine, smart dogs the townspeople liked to keep them for house dogs. Miss Balfour (the only woman there) and the boy Robert, along with a sizeable crowd of men and boys, watched as Swainston the shepherd climbed into the pen. He was a tall man with the white hair and eyelashes of an albino. His skin was white too, in spite of a life outdoors in the bleak weather of the hills; some people said that when he bled, his blood was white.

The pen already had an occupant: a mature ram with black, experienced horns, dark eyes and a thick, black penis. The ram was bristling at the smell of the pups. Swainston straddled the ram, holding it in check with his long thighs. His assistant carried a male pup into the pen, tied him by his leash to the ram's horns, then jumped back over the fence.

Some reflex in the pup's brain recognized in this woolly creature the fulfilment of his essence and sent his stumpy tail vertical with delight. He trotted forward to round up the ram.

That was when Swainston released his grip. The ram

leaped at the pup and tossed him up in the air, jabbing at the falling body with his twisted horns. The pup tried to scramble out of the way, dodging and weaving and whimpering. It was hopeless: he was tethered to his nightmare.

The process lasted only a minute. The leash became knotted in the ram's horns, and the pup, its paws no longer on the ground, was buffeted against the wall of the pen.

Now Swainston stepped in. He wrestled the ram back into immobility while his assistant disentangled the pup and gave it back to its owner; gave back, that is, a pup which for the rest of its life would avoid anything that looked like a sheep, or smelt like a sheep. That pup would grovel before lambs.

The next pup was now handed over to Swainston for the treatment, then another, then another.

One thing that impressed Miss Balfour was the way the ram was able to shut out the crowd and all other distractions and concentrate on its enemy. The pups were superior to the ram in intelligence and in generosity of spirit but that made no difference, no difference at all. They were weak. Without exception they were terrorized and broken; only the intervention of greater strength saved them.

Miss Balfour took Robert to the tamings only that one time, but she encouraged him to attend by himself in subsequent years. She knew the Carrick fathers always took the boys there, first time. It had been the custom for generations. She believed there must be something the men wanted the boys to learn from witnessing the tamings. But whenever she asked the men what it was, so that she could pass it along to Robert, they just looked at each other, uncomfortable or puzzled — perhaps at the question, or perhaps that a Carrick woman should ask it.

AND NOW YEARS later, some of these things came into Miss Balfour's mind again. Wasn't it odd, she thought, how little she remembered; as though she'd been blindfolded most of her life. When she was young, she believed that some day she'd be able to look back over her life and it would make sense. Now that she was old, looking back, she wasn't so sure a life ever did make sense.

***

"I hape ye'll mak sonse oot of yor's, Mexwall," Miss Balfour said.

During her recollections, I'd watched the tears dilute the blue of her eyes from time to time, especially when she talked about the years after the death of Alexander's wife, and her own efforts to take the woman's place. She said that even when she was sharing Alexander's bed, he'd often dream about his dead wife. Miss Balfour knew it, for when he woke from those dreams, he'd look at her with loathing.

I wanted to squeeze her shoulder and let her know I sympathized. And I would have, but the smell from her together with the sight of the mole bobbing up and down on her neck made me hold back. She seemed, anyway, resigned to her fate.

"Nee, Mexwall. Ut weesn't mont ta bay," she said. "Neethong heppens anloose it's mont ta bay." She looked very tired, but there were some questions I wanted to ask her.

"Who was that foreman you mentioned, the one at the Mine the day of the explosion?"

Her mole popped up, as though I'd surprised it.

"Eh! Yee dudn't know thet, Mexwull? Nee winder yee lock poozled. Et wiss Edom Swonstin!"

"Adam Swainston?" I was startled.

"Yees. Edom Swonstin becoom a shiphard efter the Werr." Her voice was a whisper: "Ur thengs begunning ta mock sonse noo?"

I desperately wanted to know more.

"Why was everyone so worried about Kirk talking to him?"

"Nee. Ee've tald ool ee'm poormotted ta toll." She was utterly exhausted; the blue of her eyes seemed to be fading like water paint. But she mumbled something else, and in spite of the smell, I leaned nearer to hear.

"Dud Rabart dee a gud jib an may?" she asked.

Like the others, she wanted my opinion on Aiken's version of her in his narrative.

"It was very nice," I said. Then I asked her, just out of curiosity: "But was it the truth?"

"Troth? Troth?" The question seemed to revive her a little. She answered with the ritualized answer, only slightly distorted. "Ye cun anly toll troth if ye dan't know mich."

She looked very weak now, but I kept on: "Miss Balfour. Please. Why did Aiken poison everyone?"

She was trying to turn onto her side, but made a last effort to speak; she was smiling and barely moving her lips.

"Hay gat us ell et woon foul sweep." That's what she said in her mangled way; then she fell over onto her side, and her eyes blazed up at me for a moment. If eyes are the soul of the face, then this worn face might have been a saint's. They blazed for a moment, then they turned to glass.

I shouted for the guard and he made a musical ascent. He came into the room, avoiding the piles of books, took one look at her and shook his head.

"She's dead."

I was shocked by the speed of it. Like the others, it seemed, Miss Balfour's life had run out with her string of words. As I looked down at her body, I could see that even in these few seconds death had restored some of her former beauty to her face; her skin was more opaque, the veins less visible. But her mole was still peeping out stubbornly, and I couldn't leave her like that. I pulled the collar of her nightdress up to cover it, then I wove my way through the books to the door.

"The sergeant dropped by a half-hour ago," the guard said. "He told me Sentinel Hogg's dead. There aren't many left now. We'll soon be getting out of here."

I went out onto the landing. The wind had died down during the last hour, and now a light fog had taken over. I tried to take a deep breath; but the fog seemed to be that bitter smell made visible, and I gagged on it.

I went down the stairs, and down the scale, too. The last note was a dismal bass. I walked along the alley and through the Green, avoiding looking towards the Keep, or the Pharmacy or the antique store. I was glad I didn't meet anyone as I set out up the road to the barracks, walking as fast as I could.

That night, when Reeve Blair came to my hut, he sat on the hard wooden chair and I perched on the edge of the sink hole that was my mattress. The atmosphere of that bare room appeared quite monastic to me. When he had listened to my day's tapes, he, the confessor, asked for my impressions; and I, the novice, complied while the radiator hummed its mantra, an invocation to the god of warmth. My confessor heard me without a word, but I needed words from him.

"How much of all this did you know before I came here?"

"Rumours on top of rumours. Mysteries on top of mysteries." The magic word "mystery" was meant to comfort me, but I wasn't comforted. He saw that, and said his credo. "I believe in you, James. I believe that if you don't find out what happened here, nobody else will. I believe nobody else will ever be given the chance."

"Mmmmmmmmm," hummed the radiator.

I told him how saddened I was by the deaths of Anna and Sentinel Hogg and Miss Balfour. Especially Anna's.

"James," he said, "tonight you deserve something." He got up and poured me a glass of whisky from the unopened bottle I'd brought with me. I sipped from the glass for a while and felt better.

Although it was always hard to tell with Reeve Blair, his face seemed to soften, and certainly his voice did, even more than usual.

"I know you liked Anna, James, and I can't say I blame you. You no doubt think I'm too dedicated to my profession to have any time for women. What was it you called me — a cabalist? Or you think a man in a job like mine, where there's so much seediness and horror, wouldn't be able to fall in love. Isn't that what you think? We often hear it said about our profession. And it's true some of us are contaminated. But not all of us. Not by any means. Sometimes, seeing so many awful things can make you appreciate love and beauty all the more. By the time I was your age I'd served two years in one of the worst slum areas of the Capital. I'd seen things you've only seen in nightmares. But that didn't stop me from falling in love for the first time."

REEVE BLAIR'S LOVE STORY

(transcribed from tape and condensed by me, James Maxwell)

He was twenty and had returned to the Academy of the Laws for a refresher course. He knew Veronica only by sight — she was a waitress at The Copper Cafe, a small restaurant in one of those imposing terraces half-way between his hotel (he had taken a room in The Thistle) and the Academy. He went to the cafe each night for a final cup of coffee before turning in. Veronica was a small, black-haired woman with prominent cheek-bones; she was quick moving and quick talking. But she was not young. That is to say, he himself was young then, and she did not seem young to him. When she became used to seeing him at her tables at night, they began to exchange a few words (she liked talking — she was a sociable woman). He discovered she was in her mid-forties and had worked as a waitress in bars and cafes in the Capital all her life. She'd been divorced for ten years and had a daughter who lived in the South of the Island.

"She's about the same age as you," she said.

Who knows how it was Reeve Blair fell in love with her? All he understood at first was that he looked forward more and more to his visits to the cafe each night, and to his nightly chats with Veronica during quiet periods — the cafe was most often quiet at night. What he liked so much (or so he thought) was just the conversation, uncontaminated by any kind of sexual complication. He looked upon her, he supposed, as a mother-figure replacing the real mother he'd lost so long ago in the War. She looked upon him, he supposed (he did a lot of supposing at first), in much the same way as she would her own child.

Even when he decided to ask her out for the first time, he was sure his intentions were purely amicable. He was not a gregarious man and had never had friends: now he had a friend. He thought of Veronica as "a friend." He liked the idea. She accepted his invitation, and they arranged to meet outside The Copper Cafe one night when she finished work early.

She was waiting for him when he arrived. She was wearing a little make-up and through her open coat (it was a fine evening and quite warm in the Capital) he could see a black silk dress and white pearls round her neck. He had only ever seen her in the drab uniform of her trade. Now, he suddenly realized what he hadn't noticed before — that she was beautiful.

"Veronica," he could hardly speak. "You look marvellous."

She smiled, took his arm, and they set off down the street.

From that night onwards, he no longer thought of Veronica as a mother-figure. He began to desire her as he'd desired other much younger women before. And in course of time, he took her to his room in The Thistle one night after a movie. Even though he'd never spoken to her about his feelings, he kissed her and she didn't resist. Nor did she resist when he took her hand and guided her towards the bed. But when he began to undo the buttons at the back of her dress, she pulled gently away from him.

"Just a moment," she said. She went over and switched off the light, then came back to him.

"Why did you switch it off?" he said. "I wanted to see you."

In the dark she hugged him.

"Please," she said. "I don't mind going to bed with you. I want to. But I don't want you to see my body. Please don't ask me."

So after that, he didn't ask her any more. And it didn't

matter to him. When they made love that night, and on all the other nights after, he adored her small body in the darkness with his hands and his kisses, and she wrapped herself around him with a fierce energy.

For a period of months, he was happier than he'd ever been in his life. He was in love, he was in love, and life was a miracle. He was not only in love — he wanted to marry Veronica. He asked her and she said no. She wouldn't discuss it. When he tried to ask her again, she said he would ruin everything.

One night, in his room in The Thistle, after they'd made love — she'd been very silent throughout — she went to the bathroom and was in there for such a long time, he became worried. So he slipped out of bed and went over to see what was wrong.

The bathroom door was slightly ajar and the light was on. He could see her standing looking at herself in the long mirror: her figure was good, but her breasts had stretch marks on them from the time they were swollen with milk; a jagged caesarian scar ran across her belly (he'd felt it often with his fingers) marking the place where her daughter had emerged; and the mound of hair beneath was already grey. He looked at her face, he saw she was watching him.

When she came back to the bed, he hugged her and hugged her, but she did not respond.

"I'm sorry I looked," he said.

"It's time you saw," she said. "It's time you saw."

The next night when he went to meet her, a new waitress was working there. Veronica had quit her job, she said. She had left her apartment too, and left town.

It was not easy to disappear on the Island, so he tracked her down quite easily. She'd gone South by train, and found a job in a bar at a hotel in a sunless resort by a grey sea. He took a few days away from the Academy and went to see her. He sat on a bench on the sea-wall in front of the granite-faced hotel she worked in, and waited. It was a cool, windy day and the beach was deserted except for gulls.

At about two in the afternoon, she came out through the swing door. He rose and went to meet her.

"Veronica!" he said.

She showed no surprise at seeing him.

"Go away," she said.

"Please talk to me," he said.

"Go away," she said. "You don't you know how miserable I am. I allowed myself to fall in love with a man half my age. I made myself forget how you'd look at me some day and hate me."

"Age doesn't make any difference to me," he said. "I love you."

"Yes, you're in love, that's why you can't see. Young men never do," she said. "I love you too, but love hasn't made me blind. I don't want my happiness to depend on a love that won't last. It'll be too hard to bear. I've learnt before how to be happy without love; I know how to do it, and I'm going to learn again before it's too late. If you love me, go away."

"Please," he said.

Her face became passive, sullen, as though she hated him.

"No," she said. "I wish I could hate you for what you're putting me through. Go away."

———◆———

"You know, James," said Reeve Blair, "you're the only person I've ever told about Veronica. I've loved other women since, but not as much as I loved her. She was in love with me, but she rejected me. She didn't trust me because I was young."

I was flattered that Reeve Blair had confided in me and I was astonished at this revelation of a side of him I'd never dreamt of. That was my fault again, of course — I'd been taken in by his stern appearance. From that night onwards, no matter how ascetic he seemed, I never forgot how he'd revealed his humanity to me.

The next morning I was more than slightly hung over, I was so unused to drinking even small amounts. At eight-thirty, I made my way down the road to the town. The eastern sky was just slightly ajar, and overcast. It was a typical Carrick gloom, but today I appreciated it: my eyes weren't ready for light yet.

In the town, I couldn't see any movement on the streets around the Green. The sentries in the doorways of various buildings were just ominous shapes, no more human than the three stone figures on the Monument. The windows and doors of Anna's store were barred with two-by-fours.

I turned right, along the cobblestone lane, strumming the hedge that lined it till I reached the dark house.

Symmetrical iron spikes that were meant to be ornamental stuck up out of the garden wall.

I knocked on the door and it felt like lead against my knuckles. The soldier who opened it looked me over for a moment as though he were surprised to see me. I told him I had an appointment and he let me in and pointed me up the mahogany panelled staircase, just past the open door of the study with its tall bookcases. On my right was a wooden sign on a closed door:

SURGERY
WAITING ROOM

As I climbed the stairs, I recognized the acrid miasma that seemed to rise out of the plush carpet. I hardly breathed till I got to the landing. From there I could see a panelled corridor and six doors. A nurse came out of one of them; she was a bitter-faced woman with a stick body that leaned to her left side. Unlike the soldier, she didn't seem surprised to see me.

"You have one hour," she said. "He's only stayed alive to talk to you." She edged past me (her body was made for passing) down the stairs. I switched on my tape-recorder and went into the room she'd come from.

Doctor Rankin was sitting up in a four-poster bed. His room was panelled in mahogany. The only window was closed tight, the room was warm, the smell was strong and sour. On the bedside table under the lamp, I could see a copy of Aiken's manuscript with a pair of silver rimmed half-glasses lying on top of it.

"Good-morning," I said, for he hadn't noticed me. "Doctor Rankin?"

He looked over and smiled.

"Good-morning to you, turd face."

I was surprised to hear that greeting from a virtual stranger — who wouldn't? But Reeve Blair had warned me in advance that this was the way the poison had affected the doctor: his conversation was peppered with childish insults he seemed quite unaware of.

So I said nothing, but looked him over carefully. His head was small and his hair was iron grey and thick for a man who must have been in his seventies. He wore black pyjamas that seemed to be made of silk.

"I'd offer you a glass of something, pisspot; but I no longer have a maid. She died last week." He had a thin voice, but it was full of energy; and when he smiled, he exposed yellow teeth that matched his eyes.

I wondered why Aiken had been in such awe of him. Whatever he'd been once, he was now a small man, dying.

"You've spoken to the others, have you, tottyhead? You think you understand all kinds of things now?" His tongue protruded through his small mouth, reminding me of a plug in the vent of a barrel. "What if I were to tell you you don't understand much, thickwit?"

Most of these insults were delivered with the most polite intonation. But now the conversation changed direction like a crab, and his voice if not his language became more brusque. "Enough chatter. I don't have much time and I have so much to tell about the Grubachs and about Robert's mother; so listen carefully, cabbageface."

I looked as attentive as possible, and he began his account.

"Those Grubachs. What a pair of duckleheads. Can you imagine how weird they seemed to us when they first came to Carrick?"

THE TESTIMONY OF DOCTOR RANKIN

(transcribed from tape and condensed by me, James Maxwell)

They had fled from the Continent early on in the War and settled in Carrick. They became his patients, so he got to know them well. Helena Grubach was a tall, stooped woman with jet black hair. She was in her forties and Jakob in his sixties. They spoke their adopted language in an awkward, stilted way, choking on some of its formations. In Carrick, where family names had been the same for centuries, and were worn smooth like rocks in a stream, their foreign name demanded mockery ("Hey, Grubach. When did you grow back?" the children would call out).

In his own country, Jakob had been a professor of history and a collector of antiques, following in the Grubach family tradition. But in the years before the War, his version of history was proclaimed officially unacceptable and the systematic persecution of his family began.

The ceremonial rites used in such torment were traditional and prescribed: the maledictions, the spitting, which progressed to the the breaking of windows, and would have become, in time, the breaking of limbs, and the final immolation. Before these last could happen, Jakob joined the Resistance. In the course of a violent year, he learnt some very unacademic skills: how to set booby-traps and mine bridges; and how to blow up tunnels as trains were passing through. But resistance seemed only to excite his oppressors; it became clear his only hope was to take Helena and flee. They were lucky enough to find passage for the Island on a ship whose captain's sympathy could be bought.

Carrick was the place of their exile. Helena was crushed by their misfortunes; Jakob was bitter about only one thing — that he could not strike back at his enemies: he was told he was too old to enlist in the Island's armies. So he opened a little antique store opposite the Green, and embraced the history of his new country with a passion incomprehensible to Doctor Rankin, with whom he often discussed it. For, in spite of everything, Jakob still believed in history. He believed that to possess a country's past was almost the same as possessing the solid earth of it. He wanted his adopted country's history to be a good history, the kind a good man could fit his life into. He hauled Helena through the dank museums of the Capital. The Grubachs became intimate with the rubble of medieval abbeys and the ivied shells of ruined castles. They made pilgrimages over rough fields to the sites of ancient battlefields — even while new battlefields were being inaugurated daily, abroad.

In the course of these historical researches, Helena discovered she was pregnant, much to their delight.

They were also delighted when, just about that same time, their best friend in Carrick, Alexander Aiken, the Pharmacist, told them his wife was expecting a child. Alexander, naturally, was delighted.

All that delight.

Doctor Rankin already knew something Alexander did not, something that would have tempered the Pharmacist's delight.

HE REMEMBERED WELL the day Alexander Aiken's wife had shown up at his surgery. He had often wondered how she tolerated life in Carrick after the Capital. She was slim with long, fair hair, unlike the stocky, dark women of the Upland towns. She dressed stylishly, read a lot and always had an amused look in her green eyes. Doctor Rankin had noticed how she played with Alexander the way a cat plays with a mouse; he expected any minute to hear the crunch when she reached her husband's backbone.

So, that morning when she appeared at his surgery and said she thought she was pregnant, he had to restrain his excitement. He asked the routine medical questions and she answered, smiling in her slightly patronizing way. He took tests and told her he'd be in touch.

The results of the tests arrived a few days later, and they were positive. He phoned and told her to come to the surgery at three o'clock. He made sure hers was his only appointment.

He was sitting with a medical journal in the surgery when, promptly at three, he heard her knock at the door. His maid showed her into the waiting room. She was wearing a fur coat against the February chill. He shut the waiting-room door behind her.

"Come with me," he said.

He led her into the surgery. A fire was burning in the fireplace, as it always did, winter and summer, for he disliked the cold. He locked the door and turned to her, his arms folded.

"Let's have a look at you."

She was standing in the middle of the room, looking puzzled.

"Is there anything wrong? Did you get the results of the test."

"Remove your clothes."

He could see he was making her uncomfortable. Nonetheless, she began to take off her clothes, and he watched, admiring as he had in his previous examination of her, the long legs and smooth white skin and full breasts.

"Lie down." He indicated the examination table. She climbed onto it awkwardly, her body reflected in the mirror that hung behind the table, and lay on her back.

He walked slowly over to her and touched her bare shoulder.

"You have very good skin."

She was looking at him, that supercilious smile quite gone from her face. He massaged the shoulders then moved his hands down to her breasts. He squeezed gently. Her body stiffened, but, still the patient, she tolerated his touch.

He moved his hands further down, feeling the curvature of her rib cage and the swell of her belly. She endured his hands, though he could feel the tension in her. His left hand stayed on her breast, and his right hand strummed through her fair pubic hair and slid over her groin.

Only then did she begin to resist. "What are you doing? Let me up."

She was struggling now, her thighs tight round his hand.

"Let me go, let me go!"

She was sobbing now as he held her down.

"Who's the father?" he hissed at her.

She kept struggling, crying out.

"Let me go!"

He was breathing hard now too.

"It wasn't Alexander," he hissed.

Her thighs still gripped his hand, but she stopped struggling. She was silent now, just lying there, panting. That excited him tremendously, as it always did.

"Your beloved husband had mumps when he was twenty-five. He's quite infertile. Understand? He's not capable of it."

She lay now like a rabbit about to be killed; the grip of her thighs was slackening. Fear and hatred were draining out of her eyes.

"He doesn't know it. Isn't that lucky for you?" He could hear his own voice, wheedling and high-pitched.

Her muscles had loosened and he began to move his fingers around in the dryness of her groin.

"It'll be our secret."

She lay there, making no effort to escape. He took his hands away slowly. She lay still. He began to peel off his clothes. She turned her head towards the mirror and closed her eyes. He climbed onto the end of the table at her feet, and pushed her legs apart. Watching himself in the mirror, he mounted her, and he made no sound, except, at the end, when he spilled himself into her, and still looking in the mirror, groaned, "Aaaah!"

ONE FATEFUL SATURDAY her infidelity with the prisoner was discovered. Alexander came to Doctor Rankin and told him about it — he said he wanted revenge, and he made it plain that revenge on just a single prisoner at Camp Zero would not be enough to alleviate his pain. He wanted to eliminate them all, and he had already enlisted the help of his friend, Jakob Grubach, who saw perhaps his last chance to strike a blow against those who had ruined his family and his homeland. Doctor Rankin couldn't dissuade them, but he did make them promise at least to wait a while. Choose your time carefully, he said, and I'll help too.

AT THE MIDNIGHT HOUR the old Mercedes drove slowly eastwards into the hills. The fog was thick and that was good, but the roughness of the road gave them cause to be afraid, mortally afraid. As they slowly neared the place where the road forked south, the fog was so thick that the right front wheel of the car went off the road, and dangled, spinning over the ditch. They sat without moving, without breathing for a long moment, then Alexander gently reversed till all four wheels were back on the road. Jakob Grubach, who understood the danger best, sat with his eyes clenched shut. Doctor Rankin was sweating despite the cold night.

After that, all went smoothly for a while till Alexander had to bring the car to an unwanted halt on an open stretch. He had to do so because of an apparition that stood right in the middle of the road in front of them — a tall young man in miner's clothes; he had white eyebrows and eyelashes and long white hair. He peered at them for a few moments, then stepped aside to let the car continue.

"That was Swainston," Doctor Rankin said. "He saw us."

Alexander said nothing but kept on driving, and slowly, slowly they moved towards their destination. After what seemed like another hour, they reached the far side of the St Giles Pond, which was invisible in the fog. At this point, the bank of the pond was also the north-east slope of the Cairn; more than a hundred feet of water rested on a layer of rock under which ran some of the worked-out tunnels of the Carrick Mine.

Alexander Aiken stopped the car, got out and opened the back door for Jakob Grubach. Alexander and Doctor Rankin watched as Jakob eased himself out, then lifted out the duffel bag he had been cradling all the way from Carrick. He began walking through the fog fifty yards to the water's edge, apprehensive in case he should stumble in the bracken. Alexander and Doctor Rankin followed. When Jakob reached the edge of the pond, he softly lowered the weighted bag down, down into the deep black water.

Then the three men ran away from the pond as fast as they could, back towards the car, for these were dangerous moments. Jakob Grubach, the creator of the bomb, had never before made one with a timer set to go off under water. He didn't know whether the water itself, or the change in pressure as the bag sank, might cause the nitro to go off prematurely.

They reached the car and waited, out of breath. Silence. After about five minutes, they knew the bag must by now have settled at the bottom. The bomb inside it was set to explode in the middle of the next morning, at the hour when all of the prisoners would be working in the lowest gallery of the Mine, deep below the St Giles Pond.

On their way down to Carrick again, Alexander Aiken drove without speaking, nursing his hatred. Jakob Grubach was talkative, elated at the thought of vengeance against those who'd forced this exile upon him. As for Doctor Rankin, now that the danger was over he felt nothing — except perhaps the sort of curiosity a scientist feels waiting for the results of an interesting experiment.

"And it worked out very well, didn't it, birdwit?"

This final question he addressed directly to me. I'd been feeling very uncomfortable in that bedroom. The smell and the heat were suffocating and so were this old man's ludicrous insults and general nastiness. It was hard to believe that his power had formerly depended upon hoarding up his silences. I wanted to get away from that room and from him, but I also wanted to understand more clearly some of the things he'd said.

"You say you told Alexander Aiken and Jakob Grubach to choose the time for their revenge carefully. Am I right in assuming you decided the time was ripe when you heard about the deaths of the Carrick men at the Mord River Bridge?"

Doctor Rankin's bulging eyes bulged so much I thought they might burst out of their sockets.

"You've almost got it, addlepate. Except for one thing. The time never was ripe. Do you understand what I'm saying, numbskull? THE — TIME — NEVER — WAS — RIPE." He spat this out and paused for breath. When he spoke again, his words were quiet, but clear and precise, like arrows whistling past my ear. "As a matter of fact, Alexander Aiken and Jakob Grubach blew up the Carrick Mine *the day before* the deaths at the Mord River Bridge." His face was triumphant.

What could I say? I sat there stunned at the opaqueness of the past. I'd made up a cause and effect that was understandable and convenient. And quite wrong.

Doctor Rankin saw how bewildered I was.

"Don't be such an innocent, doodleprick. All Alexander did was to anticipate Carrick's need for vengeance by one day. He and Grubach killed the prisoners from Camp Zero for their reasons. A day later when the news arrived about the deaths of the Carrick men at the Mord River Bridge, all of the townspeople had their reasons. A bit belated, but what's a day between friends, eh, rattleskull? Fate must be allowed a sense of humour, too. We all agreed to let history re-write itself just a little bit."

Rain was pattering lightly on the window now, like a snare drum accompanying his words.

"Alexander's wife was no use to anyone from then on. After the birth of the boy, she died from . . . complications." He looked at me to make sure I didn't miss the implication, and he grinned feebly. "I made out the death certificate."

His face was like a skull, for he was mortally tired — a vampire with a withering heart.

"So this is really the truth, at last?" I said.

"Truth, chowderhead? Truth? Telling truth is only possible if you don't know very much."

How many times I had heard that in Carrick!

He was still speaking, but his voice had faded so much I could barely make out what he said: "Now how could a Southerner like your friend the Reeve be expected to understand something as simple as that?"

Another, harsher voice behind me interrupted.

"So you're still alive yet?"

The nurse with the angular body was scrutinizing him. There was no telling from her thin face how much she'd heard; hers was a face made for absorbing all human behaviour, with equal distaste.

Doctor Rankin had slumped badly. I didn't want to see another one of the townspeople die, not even this one; and I needed to escape from the smell — it was so strong it was making my eyes water. I rose and started to put on my coat. He was staring up, watching me with his bulbous eyes, as I asked my last questions.

"Where does Kirk come into it? Why did Robert Aiken poison everyone?"

His smile was ghastly.

"I mustn't talk about that. Aiken'll tell you. He did a good job of me in his document, didn't he?" He said this in a loud whisper. "I saw how afraid you were when you came in." Then, as though he'd been saving the words up for his final attack on me, or maybe wanted rid of what remained, he sputtered out: "Stinkpot! Bumbelly! Scumbucket!"

That seemed to perk him up, but I left without another word. I didn't find him even the least bit funny any more.

When Reeve Blair came by in the evening, I played him my latest tape.

"What a weird old man he was," I said afterwards. "He was silly and horrible at the same time. But at least we know it was Alexander Aiken's idea to kill the prisoners for revenge, and that it was Jakob Grubach that made the bomb. But that was all in the past. It doesn't explain what's been happening here in Carrick in the last few weeks. Or does it? Sometimes I feel as though I know a lot. Other times, I feel as though these people have set us a test that can't be passed."

The Reeve was at his most comforting.

"Don't distress yourself. It'll all come out. It would be too easy if we had skeleton keys to other people's minds. You've done everything you were asked to do, and much more than I ever could. They trust you." There was admiration, if not a trace of envy in his voice.

"Reeve Blair," I said, "Before I talk to Aiken, shouldn't I talk to some of the other townspeople, like Mitchell or Cameron?"

"You can't, James," he said, "for one simple reason. They're dead. Nearly all the townspeople are dead. Anna and Sentinel Hogg and Miss Balfour and Doctor Rankin are the only ones who would agree to talk to you. It's really a miracle they lived long enough."

A miracle, I thought. Yes, I suppose it might be a miracle. A miracle in a madhouse.

"But everything's still so vague," I said. "If only we had more details."

"In my profession, and in yours, too many details may not necessarily be good," he said. "With too much detail, things can begin to blur, and look like everything else."

That was an axiom he repeated several times while we were in Carrick. One day in my hut I asked him, in all innocence, how he came to have so many unusual theories — unusual to me, at least. For an answer he gave me a long lecture on the complexities of criminal theory — perhaps it revealed something about his own position too.

REEVE BLAIR'S LECTURE ON CRIMINAL THEORY

*(transcribed from tape and condensed by me,
James Maxwell — as well as I could understand it)*

He himself had been an innocent till he was appointed Lecturer in the Academy of the Laws, specializing in criminal theory.

172

He'd spent a very enjoyable five years as a Junior Sentinel in the disreputable heart of the Old Town, walking its labyrinthine passageways, applying his mind to the mysteries. But he'd been one of the top students when he'd been at the Academy and had known it was only a matter of time before his superiors called upon him to take a teaching post.

If it hadn't been for the memory of Veronica, he wouldn't really have minded being back at the Academy. The buildings were in the New Town — though it was over a century old now — an area of elegant town houses and geometrically circular terraces. To walk through it, to work in it, was to become part of a wonderful mandala that soothed and sustained him.

But things had changed even in the brief years since Reeve Blair had been a student. The classical architecture of the Academy's buildings — symbols of order and certainty — had become a camouflage for an intellectual ferment within: the traditional theories of criminal investigation were being challenged; indeed they were already regarded as obsolete in some progressive quarters.

Reeve Blair had made himself a master of the centuries-old approach: first, analyse the crime; second, examine the scene of the crime; third, speculate on the motives; fourth, search for clues; fifth, interrogate the suspects; sixth and last, construct a profile of the criminal.

This time-consuming and frequently ineffective methodology was now openly rejected by certain revolutionary theorists who had been teaching and proselytizing at certain institutions on the Continent. As the new man at the Academy of the Laws, Reeve Blair was obliged to familiarize himself with the new theories; when he began to study them he was startled at how radically they deviated from the tradition.

The originator of the revolt was a man named Frederic de Nossurre. In his treatise, *A Course in General Criminology*, he set the world of criminal theory on its ear by the simple statement: "the nature of a crime is totally arbitrary and requires new systems of analysis." These systems could only come into being, he suggested, if the very language in which the investigator described the crime was itself subject to scrutiny. He proposed that an altogether new set of terminology be introduced, built around the triad: CRIMINIFIER — CRIMINIFIED — CRIME. For Nossurre, the criminal was the hero of his own crime; clearly, the narrative of a crime must acknowledge that basic fact, not distort it to accommodate the investigator.

Some of Nossurre's followers, such as Vincent Lotsachik, went further and called for a formal structural analysis of crimes, to establish "a system of differences" (the phrase he used in his major work, *A Theory of Crime*). Lotsachik intuited that a master criminal's genius lies in his ability to make "familiar" crimes "unfamiliar" — in this way, the criminal certainly prolongs the investigation, but, in a perverse (or not so perverse) way, gives enormous pleasure to the investigator who enjoys the intellectual challenge and apparent intricacy of the variation. A structural analysis would identify these "unfamiliar" crimes and indicate their place within the archetypical history of crime.

A disciple of Lotsachik, Rollo Jacobite, in *Fundamentals of Crime*, bewailed the lack of objectivity that bedevilled the field. He believed that "investigators have been befuddled by censorious, subjective doctrines. No manifesto, foisting the investigator's own tastes and opinions on a crime, may act as a substitute for an objective, scholarly analysis." He built upon Lotsachik's theories and stipulated a "poetics of crime," pointing to various recurrent types of structural metaphor or metonymy. The tropes appear not just in crime but in a variety of human acts, thus linking them together. He hypothesized the now classic illustration:

Judge: The accused has been found guilty of murder.

Defence: The accused is no more a murderer than you are. Haven't we all killed things in our lives — a mosquito, let's say, or a butterfly? When we walk across a lawn do we not maim or kill a thousand vegetable and insect life forms?

Judge: The comparison lacks validity.

Defence: On the surface, yes. But in a much more profound, metonymical way, we are all killers of sentient beings; we've simply made different choices than the accused about what we kill.

While many admired Jacobite's approach, a new group of theorists arose who challenged this entire structural approach to the theory of crime. Jerzcy Gonnade, in his *Figurations in Criminology*, was their leader. He contended that: "the ideological prejudice of valuing structures at the expense of substances overestimates their explanatory value." Gonnade felt that the *meaning* of a crime was of fundamental importance.

Merely analysing the crime, finding the criminal, perhaps even obtaining a confession from the criminal in no way explained the crime. He posited the famous case of the bookstore robber:

A robber robs two bookstores in the same area of the city, using the same *modus operandi*. He is arrested and confesses to both robberies. In one, he admits, he simply robbed the till — a crass, mercenary act. In the other, he says he found the till empty; so he browsed through the bookcases, and filled his sack with a stack of valuable pornographic books which he intended to sell later.

In each case, Gonnade suggests, the robber's motive is of little importance. But the implications of his actions may be momentous. The first robbery is a run-of-the mill corroboration of what is universally known: that money is an attractive commodity in our society. But the second robbery is of great interest, from Gonnade's perspective: an untrained representative of the lowest levels of our society is able to recognize and appreciate the merit of what we may call, for the purposes of argument, works of art. Surely, argues Gonnade, it is these revelations ("the *meanings*" of the crimes) that ought to be the focus of our studies.

After Gonnade, the theoretical scene became even more complex. Iago Longlac, for instance, in *The Psychotic*, argued that "criminal acts are structured like a language, and that language may mean one thing to the criminal, but quite another to the investigator." The knifing of a victim may be, for example, in the mind of the investigator, merely another act of violence. But in the criminal's mind the knife itself may be a phallic symbol, and the act of stabbing a penis thrust. The gender of the criminal who performs the act may, therefore, be all-important, or not important to one, or the other (that is, to the investigator or the criminal); or even to a third — that is, to the (all-but-forgotten) victim.

Jasper Dorraymi was the culminating figure among these new theorists. He concluded his great opus, *The Crime and the Difference*, with this incisive remark: "I embrace a world of crimes without fault, without truth and without origin, which is offered to our active interpretation." By this, he implied that the problem with all forms of investigation before him was the investigators' assumption of the centre — a secure ground upon which they stood *outside and apart from* the crime under investigation. But there is no such ground, Dorraymi said. Every crime depends upon its investigator as much as the investigator upon the crime — like the legs of twin compasses.

Consequently, Dorraymi fathered (or mothered — he relished such equivocation) a whole school of theorists who advocated the "freeplay" of the investigator. He never tired of telling his students: "Present interesting solutions! That, and only that, is your duty. Abandon the idea of relevance! The relevance of solution to crime is of no importance, no importance whatever."

Reeve Blair, after a struggle, understood the new theories fairly well. Now it happened that the Academy of the Laws had allowed female students to register for the first time, so he felt obliged to make himself familiar with those women theorists who had become prominent. Once again, he was startled at their challenges to the old theorists, and even the new male theorists. Aluna Shoulter, for example, in *Crimes of Our Own* contended that "not only is the law essentially a male invention, but so is criminal theory. Neither is relevant to the crimes of women." She and Lena Soclasz, in *A She-ory of Crime*, insisted that all ideas that emanate from male minds are necessarily tainted with gender prejudice. Even the development of certain types of crime that might express the female psyche have been hindered by dependence upon theoretical biases (Soclasz points to the absence of any serious discussion among male theorists on female vampirism, or on the recent laws regarding the eating of placenta and fetal membranes). She favoured "a proper history of crimes committed by women — the whole area has so far been neglected — and a theory suited to it, invented by women, and held in the same regard as the male majority's."

Whether the theorists were male or female, however, Reeve Blair discovered a unanimity among them on one matter — a principle they called "The Death of the Criminal." In brief, these theorists claimed that too much attention had been paid, in the past, to such criminal figures as Jeff the Ripper, the Northern Strangler, and even quasi-mythical criminals like Robinsky the Hood. To devotees of theory, such criminals and even their crimes ought to be incidental. The major theorists themselves ought to be considered the real stars of crime.

At that point, I suppose because I hoped the lecture was over, I said, "Very interesting, Reeve Blair."

But that only stirred him on further.

"When I started that first term's teaching at the Academy," he said, "it was hard to find anyone interested in investigating actual crimes. The apprentice Sentinels sat all day in the cafeteria arguing over the pros and cons of the various theoretical positions. Some of them had never actually met a criminal or investigated a crime. They preferred their discussions of 'The Hermeneutics of Crime,' 'Crime and the Exegete,' 'The Typology of Crime,' 'Criminal Aesthetology' and that type of thing. Do you remember when the Motel Paradiso affair hit the headlines, James? Those students at the Academy spent hours debating the ins and outs of that fiasco — they wanted me to offer a series of lectures on it. Even though everyone knew it was only an invention of the man whose pseudonym was Ezra Stevenson."

Of course I'd never heard of the Motel Paradiso affair; but I didn't want him to start in on that. So I just nodded.

"And while they sat arguing in the cafeteria," Reeve Blair continued, "rape and robbery went on the way it always did, even in the New Town — even just outside the Academy walls. The criminals had no interest in the niceties of theory; they simply got on with their crimes. The public was in an uproar. Then it was discovered that one of the new theorists had collaborated against us in the War. That made some people very suspicious. They thought the Continentals had invented these new theories to corrupt us from within because they'd failed to defeat us openly on the battlefield. That was why, in due course, many of our investigators began to revert to the old, trusted methods once again."

"Well, thank goodness for that!" I said. I'd listened to him patiently and thought he'd agree with my comment. But he shook his head.

"As a matter of fact," he said, "I once heard Dorraymi lecture, and I have to admit there was a kind of beauty about his theory — an acknowledgement of uncertainty. He tried to take into account the chaos of the world. But the fact is, his theories left the Island's prisons empty." Reeve Blair's grey eyes might have been smiling. "We human beings need to believe there's a clear division between our criminals and the rest of us, don't we James? Without that assurance where would we be?"

His grey eyes, I say, may have been smiling and maybe even his mouth; or it may just have been the corners of his lips curling in their usual way to let the words slip through. I couldn't be sure. In all the time I knew Reeve Blair, I could never be absolutely sure of when he smiled.

3

Will his name be Love
And all his talk be crazy?
Or will his name be Death
And his message easy?

LOUIS MACNEICE

I woke with a headache and a dry mouth. Rain was pock-pocking on the corrugated iron roof. I forced my eyelids apart and looked over at the window. The night had given birth to a grey infant. Suddenly I was wide awake.

Today, I was to meet Robert Aiken!

Today of all days, I knew I must pull myself together. So I got up, showered and dressed, put on my coat and went outside. It was raining all right, but the hills were visible; high on the slopes I could see white streamers of what might have been snow. The mess-hall was busier than usual. A group of soldiers and nurses were sitting at a long table, eating and talking quietly. Reeve Blair had just finished his breakfast and was buttoning his coat, ready to leave. When he saw me, he came over.

"The old doctor died at midnight," he said, and waited a moment, perhaps for an expression of sorrow from me. "At this rate," he said, "there won't be any of the towns-people left alive in a few days. Except for Aiken." He glanced towards the long table. "They'll all be going home soon." He checked his watch. "I'd like to stay and

183

talk, James, but I have to go to the Capital. I won't be back till tomorrow night at the earliest." He shook hands with me. "Good luck."

The rain was slanting down heavily when I set out for Carrick at precisely twenty minutes to nine. For the first time on that morning walk, I didn't meet anyone. And for the first time when I reached Carrick, I went directly to the place I'd made a point of avoiding: the Pharmacy. Two guards were standing under the lintel, trying to shelter themselves from the downpour. One of them looked at me suspiciously, but the other moved aside and opened the door for me.

"You can see him for two hours this morning," he said, "and the same this afternoon. Orders."

I thanked him and went inside, noting the surgical weaponry in the window; it didn't look pleasant. Inside, my eyes and my nostrils worked in harmony. One sense assured me this place was indeed a small country pharmacy with the long, wooden counter, the old-fashioned till, the high shelves of bottles and drawers, the rotary of dusty sun-glasses (in Carrick!), the aisle lined with cough mixtures and aspirin and shampoos. The other sense agreed: it sniffed out disinfectant, ether, cloves, soaps.

And traces of a slightly bitter smell — one that didn't belong in any pharmacy.

I walked to the back and climbed the creaky stairs, heartbeat by heartbeat. I reached the top and paused for a moment, both to calm myself and to switch on my tape-recorder.

"Ah, Maxwell."

The voice startled me so much I almost dropped the machine.

"Is that . . ."

"Yes. Aiken. Robert Aiken. It's nice to meet you."

I could see him now, sitting on the couch in the unlit living-room.

"Come in and take off your coat." His voice was rich and pleasant — he was a man in perfect health, Reeve Blair had assured me he suffered from none of the quirks brought about by the poison. I couldn't make out his face, only the outline of a head and thinning hair in front of the window. Through it I could see the trees on the Green and the Monument. I took off my coat and left it over the balcony railing.

"Sit in the armchair. It's comfortable," he said. He reached out and turned on a floor lamp; then he leaned back and we looked at each other.

Immediately, I couldn't help but notice how alike we looked in spite of the difference in our ages. He had the same thin face, and the same green eyes as my own. He was even dressed the same as I was for this day: a white shirt open at the neck, black trousers, black shoes. He could see what I was thinking.

"Yes, I've watched you several times from the window. Like father and son, I told the Reeve. Didn't he mention it? Maybe he thought you wouldn't like that." He had a strong jaw and prominent cheek-bones and when he smiled, even his smile was very like mine. "I told the Reeve the resemblance is caused by the way we pronounce our words in the North of the Island. It forces our jaws into the same shapes."

I smiled, but I couldn't help feeling I'd lost a great advantage: he'd be able to see through my masks as easily as if they were his own. Indeed, just then, he asked me if I'd like coffee.

"I've just had one," I said, and tried to look as earnest as I could; but from the way he smiled at my answer, I knew he could tell I was afraid to drink anything he had to offer. He just sat there on the couch smiling at me, with his legs crossed and his arms folded — looking less like a man accused of heinous crimes than a courteous, good-humoured host trying to make a guest feel at ease.

"I'm not offended, Maxwell," he said. "I understand how you feel. You want to stick to business, so let's get on with it. Did you interview Anna, and the Sentinel, and Miss Balfour, and Doctor Rankin?"

"Yes," I said.

"So far so good," he said. "But you must still be wondering what's going on here." He stood up and began pacing in front of the couch. "It all began a long way back, as you know. It's very hard to talk about the past, for you never know quite when it's permissible to think of it as past. It's a bit like ink spilt on blotting paper: you can't be sure where the stain will stop spreading."

As he spoke, I tried to see his own written narrative in him. He didn't seem at all sinister, here in the flesh: if anything, he was a very urbane murderer. He glanced towards the window and the Green outside.

"This isn't a very lovable place, is it?"

I presumed he meant Carrick, ringed round by bleak hills and scoured by a wet cold wind; but he may have meant the entire world. He didn't wait for me to answer.

"Still, it's a place to learn your trade. It was famous once for its craftsmen and its Festival — the Reeve told me you'd read those pages about the Festival of the Mysterium. I sent them because I thought you should know we were once part of a great tradition. They stopped holding it here centuries ago, I don't know why. But even when I was a child, Carrick still had a festival of the more usual type — a winter festival. Perhaps that's where I should begin. Yes, I'd like to begin there." He took a deep breath. "Can you imagine what it was like here during the festival?"

THE TESTIMONY OF AIKEN — PART ONE

(transcribed from tape and condensed by me, James Maxwell)

Though the weather might be rain, or fog, or snow, The Stag was fully booked during the festival. Farmers from outlying areas and even visitors from the Capital reserved rooms long in advance. The trailers and tents of the performers filled the Green.

Robert loved it all: the crowds, the ominous creak of the Ferris wheel above all other sounds, the carousel horses with their coats of glossy paint and their bold eyes, the demented waltzer, the game booths with their gypsy barkers. And their licit violence: the children of Carrick could swat with mallets the stuffed moles that popped up from their lairs; or shoot bows and arrows or pellets at the imitation ducks and rabbits that paraded before them. Each afternoon, they could watch the training sessions of two flabby professional boxers who returned each year, flabbier than ever; but when they stepped into the ring, their element, they were suddenly transformed into graceful and deadly machines.

The freak show always returned too. It was not permitted in some villages, but was a favourite with the men and boys of Carrick. Robert's father rarely attended, but urged the boy to do so. The keeper was a muscular gypsy of about seventy; before intermissions, he would bind heavy iron chains (the audience could check them) around his chest, and snap them with a deep exhalation and a smile. After that, he would turn a tap bored into a bottle tree and sell the sap. He said it was a magical tree he had bought in Australia; but the juice of it smelt very like Scotch whisky.

Robert could never see enough of the other acts the gypsy brought to Carrick: the male Siamese twins who danced reels together, and who, at the end would raise their shared tunic to show the rope of flesh and arteries that joined them — at the heart; a fat man who could outpull three straining Clydesdale horses in a tug o' war; a beautiful French woman with eight breasts (for an extra fee she would allow spectators to come to her trailer and feel for themselves her extravagant deformity); and, from the South Sea island of Oluba, a spikey haired man with bloodshot eyes who could eat broken glass and lighted cigarettes.

One year, as a special treat, the gypsy brought with him a contortionist who could wind himself like a snake into a transparent jar or fold himself inside a medium-sized suitcase. That astounded Robert and the other children. But the contortionist had a yet more amazing feat: he could bend over and put his lips round the tip of his own penis. The audience applauded wildly when he showed how easily he could do it; but the contortionist himself looked sad in spite of his marvellous gift.

The most popular of all the artistes, however, were two elderly miners from the nearby hill town of Muirton. They had each lost a leg in an accident that killed and maimed half the town's miners. One of them had lost his right leg, the other his left. They had discovered, after a time, that if they clung together, they could walk co-operatively like one very large man with widely placed legs. So they had persuaded a surgeon to sew their bodies together at the hip. Thus artificially transformed into Siamese twins, they seemed much happier than the two who had been born linked.

Robert particularly liked to watch the artist who attended each year. He was a thin man with long fingers. He would sketch anyone with enough nerve to sit for him (no one ever sat for him twice). A crowd usually gathered round to see him practise his trade. He would study the face of his subject for a few moments, then begin to draw with great speed. His pencil would reveal characteristics his sitters never knew they possessed or had managed to keep hidden — sometimes the despair, sometimes the darkness in them. During one festival, Kennedy's wife was his subject. When he had finished, she complained that the woman in the sketch looked crazy.

"That isn't a true likeness of me. Have you no interest in truth?"

The artist looked around and saw a bucket full of sand nearby; he took a handful of the sand and let it sift through his long, thin fingers.

"That is truth," he said.

The favourite of Robert's father was a wizened sailor, his body like a cabin trunk, tattooed with the names of ports he had sailed to all over the world. This sailor would demonstrate the art of tying knots; as he tied each one, he would tell the story of how and where he had learnt it, and what was its use. Without even looking, he could tie running bowlines, stuns'l bends, middleman's knots, and a great variety of half-hitches, inside clinches, bends and stoppers.

The knot that took Robert's fancy most of all was the carrick bend (he presumed wrongly — as did all the children — that it was called after their own landlocked town). This bend, the old man said was one of the most beautiful of knots and it had only one purpose: to join two ropes together. Beautiful it was, he assured the audience, but dangerous. Even an expert like himself could never tell, just by looking, whether it had been tied properly. No experienced sailor would trust a carrick bend unless he had tied it personally. His own best friend, when they were shipmates rounding the Horn in a dreadful storm, had gone overboard to his death because he had trusted his weight to someone else's carrick bend.

"Its beauty is as deceitful," the old man would always say, "as a woman's." The spectators would smile at that, but not Robert's father, Alexander Aiken.

Robert heard from another boy that the old sailor was a fake, that he had never been to sea and was really an ex-miner from another hill village. When he told his father this, he became angrier than Robert had ever seen him (as Alexander grew older, he was more and more easily made angry).

"A man's life may be a lie," he said, "and his stories may be the absolute truth."

Not long after the War, festivals went out of fashion and no performers came to Carrick any more.

ROBERT GROWING UP became more and more friendly with Anna Grubach — till friendship was no longer the word for it. Her father, Jakob Grubach, bought the big house in a thicket of firs on the west side of the village. It had been the Carrick mine-owner's house, and those trees were among the few that had not been chopped down over the years to be used as props in the mine. The first time Robert spent the night at that house was on a Friday at the end of June during his fourteenth year. Alexander had gone to the Capital on business, and wouldn't be back till the next day, so the Grubachs asked Robert to come and eat with them, and stay over.

THE GRANDEUR OF THE HOUSE impressed Robert; the furniture was old, the walls were cluttered with muskets, claymores and lochabers. Anna's parents were as grand as the house. Jakob Grubach was gaunt with long, grey hair swept to one side of his head. He wore the kind of smoking jacket a nineteenth-century gentleman might have worn. As for Helena Grubach, she was a sad woman, draped with jewellery and heavily made-up; the make-up only highlighted the wounds in her eyes.

After dinner (a goulash — a meal for a foreign mouth, Robert thought), they all sat in front of a fire in the living-room, and listened to Jakob's monologue on the last four battlefields he'd visited, Helena nodding her agreement to everything he said. At eleven, the three Grubachs said good-night to Robert and went upstairs to their rooms. He himself went to the guest room, which was downstairs.

Anna came to him about midnight.

Oh, the bliss in that bed. Under the warm blankets, with no need to hurry, they whispered and fondled and groaned and surrendered.

Then came the knocking at the door!

That knock shattered their ecstasy to small pieces, and they rolled apart. A voice at the bedroom door was calling softly; it was the voice of Helena Grubach.

"Anna! Anna!" she called.

Slowly she turned the handle of the door, and pushed it open.

Robert could see her white outline in the doorway. She stood for a while watching, as though she might say something. Then she closed the door quietly and they heard her footsteps walking along the hall and up the stairs till all was silence again.

The next morning when Robert was taking his leave, Helena Grubach put her hand on his arm.

"Dear Robert. How delightful it was to have you with

us," she said gravely. "You must come and stay with us any time you like. It's so good for Anna."

HE NEVER SLEPT in that house again. By the time he and Anna were eighteen and ready to go to university, he knew their romance, painted in colours that did not exist, was over. He had persuaded himself he loved her, yet he was relieved at the thought of getting away from her. And she didn't seem to mind, either: she had never once told him she loved him. They agreed that their relationship had been too easy; love must have more to it than this. They wondered if they'd only been doing five-finger exercises in preparation for some great performance yet to come.

So they went to separate universities and saw little of each other. Robert enjoyed the memory of Anna, preserving it like a locket of hair of a dead loved one; often, when he was preoccupied with other things, her image would flicker in his mind, like the involuntary twitch of an amputated limb.

But after he graduated, he worked in the Capital for a while, met another woman and married her — a kind woman, with a softer face than the women of the Uplands. She told him every day she loved him.

For three years his marriage was relatively happy. Then the happiness began to evaporate, he did not know why: he felt like a man, after a good dinner, with the jagged edge of a bone stuck in his throat; all memory of the meal's pleasures was forgotten.

He kept these feelings to himself. But about the same time, almost as though it were a consequence, his wife was stricken with an illness and began to sicken and die. He was full of remorse, and visited her daily in the hospital. But one day, with the merciless insight of the dying, she told him not to come back.

"When you are at my bedside," she said, "I see myself already dead in your eyes."

———◆◆◆———

"She was right, Maxwell," Robert Aiken said. "She died soon after that, and I told my father I'd like to come back and live here in Carrick and work in the Pharmacy. I felt so bad about her death I burned photographs, clothing, anything that would remind me of her. My father, Alexander, never once mentioned her name. We carried on our lives just as though she'd never existed."

The only sound I heard for a moment in that upper room was the soft plop of a tap in the kitchen, pitting the silence. Aiken seemed to me at that moment the saddest of men. He had been sitting for a while and now he stood up.

"But she did exist," he said. "I actually thought I loved her when I married her. Then the world started to write itself on her soft face, and after a while, she might as well have vanished, and a stranger taken her place. It's a funny thing. I wonder if that's the problem in marriages: finding out if you can love the stranger who emerges?" He frowned at me. "But you're too young yet to be able to answer that, Maxwell. Unless only the young are capable of answering such questions." He looked out of the window at the rain still pouring down on Carrick. "I remember her only too well. Isn't it odd how we remember some things so clearly. Other memories are not so clear. All that's left of them is the knowledge they must have happened, like the light that still shines from a star that died long ago."

"What about Anna?" I asked. "When did she come back here?"

"She worked in a museum in the Capital for a while after she graduated. Then she came back to Carrick, but not because of me. Her parents died and she took over the antique store. We became friends again. She was always there when I needed her. When I was desperate, she would press herself against me like a bandage against a wound."

He looked so sad I felt sorry I'd asked about her.

"And now Anna's gone," he said. "They're all gone — Miss Balfour, Doctor Rankin, Sentinel Hogg. I shall miss them all." Suddenly he turned to me. "Did you like Anna?" He was watching me carefully.

"Yes. I did," I said. "I honestly did."

"That's good." He smiled. "She was well worth liking. You must wonder why our love, if that's what it was, dried up. But if you lived for long in a place like Carrick, you'd understand why. Lovers here get to know each other too well. They become part owners of each other. Then they begin to think: there's a world out there, and we know nothing about it. They become convinced love can't be born in a place as small as Carrick. They believe that what they feel for each other is so inbred it must be some kind of deformity. If they don't do something about it, after a while they disgust each other. Can you possibly know what I mean?"

"I think so," I said.

"Good. I'd like you to understand me," he said.

"Time's up!" called the soldier from downstairs. I rose and went to the bannister for my coat.

"Will you be back this afternoon?" Aiken asked.

"I certainly will," I said.

"Thank you," he said, smiling.

As I walked back to the barracks for lunch, I felt almost light-hearted. I know I shouldn't have. But I'd almost convinced myself, at that moment, that Aiken was one of the most pleasant and interesting men I'd ever met. I was flattered at the way he confided in me.

That was how I was at that time of my life — too easily impressed. I knew it, but what could I do? My personality was a blank canvas ready for a set of colours. Even if the painter was the perpetrator of a monstrous crime.

At one o'clock, I was back in the upper room of the Pharmacy, listening to Aiken again. He was sitting on the couch drinking coffee.

"You must have wondered by now," he said, "what the connection is between the events that happened here during the War and these recent occurrences."

"That's exactly what I'd like to know," I said.

He sipped slowly at his coffee.

"My father, Alexander Aiken, is the key. It's hard for me to talk about him; I feel as though I'm speaking with toothless gums. He died a year ago and was buried here in Carrick. His mind was ruined, but his body was healthy. Isn't it funny how sickness seems to avoid those who want to die? If a father really can die, that is, when he has a son to survive him." He carefully put down his cup on the table beside the couch. "Many of the things Alexander said and did I remember vividly. For the rest, all I can recollect are slivers of conversations, fragments of incidents." He finished his coffee and put down the cup. "Is your own father still alive, Maxwell?"

"Yes. Both my parents are."

"That's good. I'm not one of those who believes our parents destroy us. Are you?" He smiled, and what could I do but smile in return, though I wasn't sure what he meant. "I had no mother," he said, "and it must have been awful for any man as debilitated as Alexander Aiken was to be both father and mother to me. But he loved me — that I know. He did the best he could. He wanted me to survive fortune's blows and he thought it important that I learn to conceal my feelings, never allow my outer appearance to betray me." He laughed, a pleasant laugh. "I never asked him why it would be so dangerous for me to reveal myself. I was a boy, and I took his word for it. I spent hours in front of the mirror prac- tising various facial expressions — looking interested, or affectionate, or happy, whatever was required, till I could put them on any time. I suppose that's the actor's trade, but it made me feel like a trained monkey imitating human emotions."

It did occur to me that Aiken might be acting right now, for my benefit; but I put the thought out of my head. I was enjoying listening to him and I wanted to believe in him.

"As I grew into adolescence, Alexander talked to me less and less. And after a while, when I asked his advice on anything at all, he refused to give it. 'Intimate conversations are forms of nakedness that should be avoided,' he said." Aiken smiled and nodded his head. "Really, Maxwell. He said that. And he kept most of our private communications down to a few axioms of that kind. Mitchell — the owner of The Stag — had a younger sister who hanged herself. My father said to Mitchell: 'The only true last sacrament is suicide.' Wasn't that a good one? The only time he even approached talkativeness was when I told him I wanted to travel abroad for a year after university. He didn't like the idea at all. He told me right away, 'Travel is a self-inflicted wound. Some people need to travel to find out where it was they came from. But not us. We know only too well where we are.'" Aiken smiled at the memory of it. "He was really desperate, trying to persuade me to stay in the Island. He said, 'The charm of strange countries isn't very different from the charm of madness.' I didn't realize then how familiar he was with that particular terrain." Aiken wasn't smiling now. "Once, just before his mind went entirely, he said, 'We should blush at the state of the world; we should blush at ourselves for wanting to remain in it.'"

He fiddled with the coffee cup then looked up at me.

"I loved him, you know. But people here don't talk much about love, and he wasn't the kind of father you could ever say it to. But we got along well together. Visiting him in that institution was heartbreaking. In March last year they phoned me and said I must come immediately — it would be my last chance to see him alive. Can you imagine how I felt that day?"

THE TESTIMONY OF
AIKEN — PART TWO

(transcribed from tape and condensed by me, James Maxwell)

He took the early train from Carrick to the Capital. At the Eastern Station, he had to wait an hour before catching a taxi to the institution. The station was busy and he didn't much feel like standing around, thinking.

So he breasted the stream of travellers and reached the boutiques and magazine stalls and the restaurant at the far side. Above him, the station roof of ten thousand dirty glass panes kept the daylight out no less effectively than it must have done when the great steam engines belched and chugged their sooty way in and out for half a century. If the doors of the place had been large enough, if they had been thrown open, the stale air would have rushed out and the building would have collapsed with a great sigh.

As for the faces Robert Aiken glimpsed as he crossed the rotunda, if they gave away anything at all, it was the old message: we are people who mind our own business, so why don't you do the same? These city dwellers with their pale faces knew the value of giving off just the right aura of ill-will, a necessary deterrent in a hostile world.

Robert looked at the magazine racks for a while, but

could not concentrate, so he thought he might as well have a cup of coffee. He pushed open the door of the restaurant. Inside, the smell was much the same as in the rotunda. The imitation coffee, the imitation doughnuts, the imitation stew must all be tainted with staleness. The restaurant was full of people, but there was no hubbub of conversation. He found the one empty table and no sooner sat down than he knew why it was empty. Something was going on at the next table.

In Carrick, in the country he knew well, Robert would have obeyed an instinct that warned him to leave. Here, country instincts were not reliable. He was curious: he wanted to hear what the waitress, a woman whose tight curls matched her mouth, was saying to the man at the table beside his.

"This is your last warning," he heard her say. "You've been here long enough."

The man mumbled back at her, making no effort to leave.

"Right," she said. "I'm going for the manager."

Robert studied the man's back. He was wearing a brown overcoat that must have been hot in the stuffy restaurant. The coat was dirty at the collar. The man's hair was a dirty grey, long and uncombed, the pallid skin at the crown thrusting through. Everyone in the restaurant was watching when the manager, a short, angry-faced man came to the table.

"You've been here since we opened this morning," he said. "I'll give you five minutes to eat up and get out."

The customer turned to the manager and for the first time, Robert saw his face, a long, thin face, unshaven, a tall man's face; but the eyes were the eyes of Alexander Aiken, and of all those who daily awake into a nightmare world.

"I'll eat when I have the inclination." The man's voice was soft.

The manager went back to the kitchen and in a few seconds returned, this time with a burly station worker. They took the customer by the arms and began hoisting him up from his chair. The table fell over, sending scrambled eggs and coffee in the air. But they had him under the armpits and kept lifting him till he tumbled out into the aisle. They let him go — and he dropped to the floor.

Now Robert could see; everyone could see. The man's left leg stopped at the knee. He lay there on the floor, a one-legged man.

The manager and his assistant stood there uncomfortably, not knowing what to do.

"Hand me my crutches, please," said the man on the floor. His voice was still mild. They noticed then the crutches lying alongside the wall; the manager picked them up. He and his assistant helped the one-legged man upright, then they flanked him to the door of the restaurant. Silently they held the doors open while he hobbled through.

When he was outside, he moved along by the window, turned again, and looked into the restaurant. His eye caught Robert's and his lips mouthed a word at him over and over again. People at the tables nearby were watching Robert who could not help watching the long sad face, the mad eyes. He could not hear what could not be heard, softly emanating from the lips of the one-legged man, over and over; but on that day, it seemed to him, the word was: "Aiken. Aiken. Aiken."

After a while, the man at the window hobbled away, still mouthing his mantra, and Robert was able to leave the restaurant and catch his taxi.

WITHIN AN HOUR he was at the institution, in Alexander's room, and he knew the situation was hopeless. His father did not seem even to recognize him, but used him as an audience for his fearful obsessions.

"The body is nothing but a food supply for a million maggots," he told Robert. "They're camped inside of us, all our lives. Look in a mirror, and you see them skulking around just under the skin." He narrowed his burning eyes and inspected his visitor's face eagerly, not to see who he was, but to search for the maggots he was certain were in hiding there.

For the first time, Robert hoped his father would soon die and be embraced by the ultimate nothingness that was the only certainty he had ever believed in.

In the Eastern Station as he waited for his train back to Carrick, Robert was filled with a vague terror: he kept thinking he could hear the clack of crutches coming towards him on the paved rotunda. He only began to feel some sense of security when he was in the train, moving away from the Capital, and he was able to look back out of the compartment window at the Capital receding, the tall buildings with houses lying round them like the debris at the foot of treacherous cliffs.

THEN MARTIN KIRK, the Colonial, arrived in Carrick and all security disappeared.

Robert went to meet him at The Stag one night shortly before the vandalizing of the Library. As he walked from the Pharmacy round the perimeter of the Green, looking in the windows of the stores, he felt apprehensive in a way he never had before in Carrick. The night and the fog transformed even the familiar: that stuffed dog in Anna's window, the puppy with the blaze on its chest — it became a sinister, bloodstained creature; two townspeople, sitting chatting in the cafe, assumed conspiratorial postures; their faces when they looked out at Robert passing were malevolent.

He reached The Stag and went down into the bar. At the very moment he entered, the taped music stuttered and choked off. Kirk was already seated, so Robert took his drink and sat opposite him at a table by the fire. It was a very old table with layers of initials and arrows and hearts carved on top of one another, an alphabetical battlefield. Over this silent babble, he studied Kirk.

Even in the light of the bar, how much more weather-beaten Kirk's face was now than when he had first arrived. It seemed a face more at home in Carrick than Robert's own, or Mitchell's, or any of the white faces of the indoorsmen. Here, Robert thought, is a man so root-less he can make himself a native of any place in a few weeks, a man adaptable enough to be dangerous.

"Thanks for coming," said Kirk. He reached inside his jacket pocket and pulled out a wallet. He opened it carefully and extracted a photograph taken with a box camera. He handed it to Aiken. The photograph was so old it was brown and bent at the edges. In it, a group of men were lined up like a football team in front of a high fence with strands of barbed wire at the top and overhanging lights. Behind the fence rose low, indistinct hills.

"Swainston the shepherd told me about the drowning of the prisoners and showed me this photograph," Kirk said. "I have a particular interest in one of the prisoners. Let me tell you why."

DUSK WAS FALLING rapidly all over the Continent. The young woman and her husband had been on the move for hours, slinking around dreamy villages (each house with its little orchard), staying off the roads, finally entering the cool forest. It was hard to believe there was a war.

But now, a half-mile behind them, they heard what they had feared all day: the baying of wolfhounds. He held her elbow, helping her walk, for she could no longer run, stumbling over every fallen branch.

"We'll be at the river soon," he said. They were both just turned twenty, man and wife — she was fair of skin.

They emerged from the forest. Across a brief swath of grass, they saw the river, a half-mile wide at this point and sluggish.

"You go in and start swimming," he said. "Take your time and you'll get to the other side easily. I'll join you soon."

She looked at him, shocked. "No. You come with me, right now."

"It's not dark enough. I don't want them to get a shot at us. I'll attract their attention while you cross."

"No, no, no." She was sobbing, hardly able to speak. "I won't go unless you come too."

Now, in addition to the baying of the hounds, they could hear not far off the crash and snap of branches under the soldiers' boots. Darkness was still a half-hour away. He took her by the shoulders.

"Remember the baby. You must go. I promise, I'll join you later." He put his hand on the swell of her belly. "You know you must try," he said, smiling, though she could see he was afraid. He led her, still sobbing, down to the water's edge. She did not resist. He pressed her hand.

"Quickly."

The water was warm and deep within a few yards of the shore, and soon she was swimming, her skirt billowing behind her. She looked back once in mid-stroke and saw him, crouched, running back into the woods towards the terror and the dark. A few seconds later, when she swivelled to look again, he was gone.

ROBERT LISTENED but said nothing.

"I heard that story over and over," Kirk said, "when I was growing up. How she escaped from the Continent and reached the Colony by ship. How, after a few weeks the child was born."

Robert was silent.

"I was the child," Kirk said. "My parents were trying to escape from their own country. They made the mistake of wanting their child to be born somewhere in peace. But war was everywhere. In wartime, peace-lovers are more dangerous than soldiers; they are the enemies of both sides."

Robert was silent.

"My father must have been caught and forced to join the army. But my mother never gave up waiting for him," Kirk said. "The War ended, and still he didn't appear. All she had was a wedding picture — she showed me it so often I knew all the faces by heart. I knew my father's face. She died years ago."

Robert was silent.

"But none of this has anything to do with my being here," Kirk said. "I am here by chance. It was only by chance I came to Carrick to do some research; by chance I met Swainston in the hills. He told me about Camp Zero, and about the deaths at the Mine; he was the foreman the day of the explosion. He said it was no accident and he had his suspicions about who was behind it. He showed me this photograph of the prisoners and there was my father's face among them."

Robert asked a question.

"Which one do you say is your father?"

Kirk pointed to the man in the second row, the prisoner with the beard.

"I recognized the photograph," Robert Aiken said to me. "You've seen it too, Maxwell."

"The one in the newspaper article? But it was hard to make out any of the faces."

"The photograph was no clearer. But Kirk said he was sure." Aiken took a long breath. "That's all that matters. And I knew what everyone in Carrick knows: that my father was responsible for the killing of the prisoners at Camp Zero."

Oh, the patterns, the strange patterns that seemed to dictate the history of this little town! I couldn't help marvelling at the patterns as I sat in that upper room listening to Aiken — waiting for him to say what was obvious and logical. He didn't, so I did.

"Kirk may have been your brother," I said.

In the silence, the pungent smell seemed suddenly much stronger.

"Did you tell him?" I asked.

Again, he was silent for a long time. Then, "No," he said. "I couldn't have told him then, even if I'd wanted to. I didn't even know till after Kirk was dead that the bearded prisoner had been my mother's lover. It was then Doctor Rankin told me about that and about Alexander's infertility. I'd always believed the prisoners were killed to avenge the deaths of our men at the Mord River Bridge."

"What about Anna? Did she know?"

"No, she had no idea. And now that Doctor Rankin's dead, you, Maxwell, are the only other living person who knows that part of the mystery."

I wanted to make sure I'd understood.

"So Alexander Aiken actually helped kill your real father?"

He had walked past the couch and was looking out the window, so his back was to me.

"So far as I'm concerned, Alexander Aiken was the only father I ever had. I love him no matter what he may have done and I honour his memory." His voice was quiet, but he spoke with clarity and total conviction.

The soldier terminated our interview at that point.

As I walked back up to the barracks, thoughts swirled through my mind like a shoal of fish. I tried to be rational, to think carefully about all I'd heard. But it was hard to think: I knew a lot, but not enough; one minute, I was confident — then the next, I was bewildered. Out of the knot of circumstances, I was beginning, for the first time, to disentangle many of the strands that connected the past and the present. But so much was still missing that would drag these Carrick mysteries out of the shadows into the light.

I was determined that at our next meeting I'd ask Aiken to tell me more about the vandalism, and the murder of Swainston and the death of Kirk. Most important of all, I'd ask him about the poisoning of the people of Carrick. His own friends had made no effort to deny his guilt; and after all he was the only one of the townspeople who was impervious to the poison. But I didn't want to believe that Aiken was a murderer. Perhaps he was innocent of everything. I wanted him to convince me that he was absolutely innocent.

I stopped thinking about that. I preferred, instead, to reflect on the astonishing set of coincidences that led to his discovery that Kirk might be his brother. I wished deeply that Reeve Blair were here; I couldn't wait to tell him what I'd found out, what a very astute apprentice I was. And to ask him to please, please tell me what it all meant.

Something happened to me that afternoon, worth noting because it shows my state of mind at the time.

It was around two o'clock, and the wind and rain had tapered off. After sitting for a long time in my room making notes, pondering the Carrick mysteries, I needed to let off steam; so I decided to climb the Cairn. The guard at the barracks gate told me to be careful. He pointed to the streamers of fog in the clefts of the hills.

"Don't worry," I said. "I won't linger."

As it turned out, the climb was less a climb than a strenuous walk up a very steep hill. I made good time, and was at the top by three-thirty; but the fog had definitely thickened. I gave myself just a minute or two to look around.

So this was Aiken's favourite place. How beautiful the world looked from up there. The crests of the other three hills split the fog like dolphins' fins. I could make out, or maybe I only imagined, the shape of the Monolith over to the north-west, and some of the streams twisting through the moors. I could see the occasional cluster of sheep on the sides of the Cairn, but no colours. I thought, this must be how a colour-blind man sees the world.

I would have liked to stay longer, but dusk was barely an hour away, just time for me to follow the scribble of a path down again, before the fog became a tangible darkness.

I started down. The earth under me was solid for the most part, but at times it sucked at my boots, and sighed up its ancient stink.

Further down, on the brow of the moors, I noticed two birds wheeling round me with their greedy eyes. I shouted and waved my arms around my head till they flew off. I'd no idea if they were the types that would attack. In fact, I'd no idea what their names were. But I wasn't afraid really; it was seductive, in a way, to be in a place of no names, in light that was almost dark.

I plodded on as fast as I could, for I knew I couldn't be far from the gravel road. After that, it was a safe half-mile walk down to the barracks even in darkness and fog.

Just then, I heard a sound behind me, and I stopped and listened. It seemed to be a pounding noise, like heavy, rhythmic footsteps on the path. I called out: "Who's there?"

The sound stopped, with a slight echo.

I walked on, faster now. I tried not to be afraid. It might be an animal back there in the fog. But common sense seemed so fragile up there, among the hills.

I walked and walked till my boots crunched on gravel, at last, and it was as though I'd stepped across the barrier between worlds. I looked back along the path. There was no sound any more. But was that a shape? Or just a dark patch of bracken? Or a hollow in the moor?

"Who's there?" I called out towards it.

It didn't move, and it didn't answer, and I wasn't tempted to go back and look. I turned and jogged down the road, and reached the barracks in five minutes.

The sentry saw me coming out of the dark.

"Is that you?" His voice was tense.

"Yes, it's me. Maxwell."

The wedge of light from the overhead bulb showed him it really was me. He lowered his rifle:

"Was everything all right up there?"

"Yes, it was all right."

"I thought I heard a noise."

"Noise? What kind of noise?"

"It sounded like a drumbeat."

I went into the barracks. The caged bulbs were radiating above the doors of the huts. I could hear music from a radio in one hut, and deep voices from another. The curtains of Reeve Blair's window were open, but there was no light inside.

When I got into my room, I was shivering. Perhaps, for a moment, I'd glimpsed something awful, something I didn't want to know: that beauty is flimsy and unreliable, that much more profound and enduring is the power of terror and the dark. I poured myself a Scotch from my emergency bottle and drank it down. Then I went into the tiny washroom and filled the sink with hot water. I rolled up my shirt sleeves and plunged my hands in. But even though the alcohol and the hot water warmed my body, I didn't stop shivering for the longest time.

That night, I slept poorly. Around midnight, the wind began to howl and the Nissen hut's timbers groaned like a ship in a gale in the Northern Sea. I dozed on and off and I was glad when the light of dawn touched my window, even though it was a miserable, grey light.

After my morning coffee and toast in the mess-hut, I made my way down to Carrick. The soldiers on guard outside the Pharmacy were expecting me.

"You're not allowed in this morning," one of them

said. "They're doing more tests on him. Come back at two o'clock."

So I returned to my hut and began transcribing some of my tapes; they refreshed my memory and kept me busy all morning.

At two o'clock, Aiken was sitting on his couch waiting for me. He didn't seem as much at ease as he was the day before; he was wearing the same clothes and when he rose to greet me the smell from him was much stronger. He didn't offer to shake hands, and I was glad.

"In Carrick," he said, as I sat down, "it's so easy to be deceived. You must have noticed that on your climb yesterday." There was an unpleasant glitter in his eyes as he spoke, a wildness I hadn't seen before. I felt uncomfortable and hoped he was referring to the weather; at any rate, he made no more mention of the climb. He sat down again.

"This is going to be hard for me today," he said. "At times I feel the more certain things are talked about, the less solid they become — the words are like weeds growing between the really important matters. Perhaps when the crazy logic of dreams is introduced into the rational world, words are useless. Or perhaps some emotions — revenge, for example — are a million years older than any words we've invented for them." He had launched into this monologue without any preliminaries, as though no time had passed since we'd last met.

But something had passed, of that I was quite sure. The pleasant, likeable Robert Aiken of yesterday had passed. It was disconcerting for me; I felt as though I were seeing him through separate lenses of binoculars and couldn't bring the two images together properly.

"Maxwell," he said, "it's time you knew the facts about what's been going on here lately: the vandalism, the murders of Swainston and Kirk, and of course, the poisoning. I'm going to tell you everything. Isn't that what you came here for?"

I nodded.

"Let me begin by admitting quite bluntly: I'm the criminal, the perpetrator of all the acts. You might as well know that right away."

I can't say how shocked and sad I felt. That was the one thing I had hoped I wouldn't hear from his lips.

"When Kirk arrived in Carrick," he said, "I knew from the way he was searching around and from his questions that there would be trouble. I wanted the townspeople to drive him away from here. I wanted them to hate him."

I sat and said not a word as Aiken began to unveil for me, finally, the recent mysteries at Carrick.

"Can you imagine how I felt," he said, "on that first night?"

THE TESTIMONY OF
AIKEN — PART THREE

———◆━◆◆━◆———

(transcribed from tape and condensed by me,
James Maxwell)

The wind was howling and all Carrick was in bed when Robert Aiken looked out of his window at one o'clock in the morning.

He put on his coat and lifted his bag of tools. The wind was cold as he walked across the damp Green — he welcomed the whine of it among the pines covering any noise he might make. At the Monument, he could see well enough by the light from the street lamps round the perimeter of the Green to climb up onto the familiar plinth. He did not allow himself to think of falling, though the climb was harder than he remembered.

He anchored himself in position and began to swing his axe at the female. The edge bit into the lead as easily and silently as if it had been wet clay. He chipped away at her until the face was quite erased. Then he turned his attention to the two soldiers. The overhang of their helmets protected their faces, so he had to swing awkwardly, and his arm was tired by the time he had finished. At last, he lowered himself to the ground, unscrewed the plaque, and sprayed a red circle on the naked marble.

He was finished. Then he thought of one last thing. He heaved himself back up onto the plinth and with his cold chisel, made a crevice in the groin area of the woman. He hacked at one of the soldiers' bayonets till he was able to snap it off, then he wedged it into the newly made opening. When he climbed down, he was sweating. He put his tools back into his bag, and slunk back to the Pharmacy. He locked the door behind him, went up to bed and slept like a child.

"There would have been no point," said Robert Aiken, "in making my first act too subtle; that would have been like a sound directed at the deaf. I wanted the violation to seem primitive, the way children in their tantrums unleash terrible emotions: rage, pain, the lust to destroy. When I vandalized the Monument, I meant to leave an impression of passion of that sort, to frighten the people of Carrick.

"They were frightened all right, I could see that; but they didn't suspect Kirk right away, and I didn't mind. In due course I struck again, and again I chose the hours just after midnight."

HE DRESSED IN DARK clothes and blackened his face, for the moon was bright and there was no sign of fog. He put on sneakers to soften his footsteps and walked out of the town along the western road, past the marsh.

The heavy iron gate of the graveyard was ajar as he went inside. He took his hammer out of his bag, and began working his way towards the back, smashing everything he passed that caught his eye. He was surprised at how easy it was to destroy these attempts to commemorate the past. Many of the stones were so soft they crumbled at a blow, almost as though they welcomed it. The statues were the least resistant so he broke off every protrusion within reach: heads, limbs, wings. Some of the more ornamental stones he singled out for special treatment.

At one point, he hefted two of the toppled angels into an obscene posture, and made a coil of debris around them. He smeared a thick circle on the back of one of the angels with one of the tubes of lipstick he'd brought with him.

He found a dead sheep lying by the main pathway and dragged it to an empty grave. He pushed it over the edge and piled just enough dirt on it to cover it up. Then he carried some pieces of an angel onto the roadway and dropped them where a passing motorist was bound to see them. Satisfied, he headed quickly towards Carrick.

"I desecrated my own father's grave that night," said Robert Aiken, "and I felt no regret; he'd avoided crowds all his life and wouldn't have wanted to join all those others after death.

"The vandalism at the graveyard shocked the townspeople, as I knew it would. They would never have believed one of our own could have done it, and some of them now began to suspect Kirk. But still they allowed him to go about his business. When he told me he was convinced his father was one of the prisoners at Camp Zero, I knew it was time for me to act again."

IT WAS BITTERLY COLD and the fog was thick as he crossed the Green to the Library in the early hours of the morning. He wore a rubber coat and rubber gloves, and he hobbled as he walked, breathing hard from the weight of the jug. The door at the bottom of the stairs was open, as usual; he slipped inside away from the street lights, into the darkness. He climbed the wooden stairs awkwardly, holding the jug away from his body. Upstairs, through the glass door he could see quite clearly because of the night light at the desk. He smashed a hole in the glass and held his breath, for the noise was so loud he was afraid it would wake the town.

Nothing but silence.

He put his hand through the hole, turned the latch, and went inside, straight to the shelves at the far side of the reading area. He uncorked the bottle and began walking the length of the shelves, shaking out the liquid, making sure not a book was missed. When the jug was empty, he made a crude drawing and a circle. Then he picked up the jug, coughing a little as the fumes snaked down his throat.

He stopped for a second at the door: he could hear the books hissing. So he went down the stairs and quickly made his way across the Green.

"For a man who loves books," said Robert Aiken, "destroying them was a very difficult act. The memory of the hissing noise tormented me for days. I convinced myself it was a necessary act to eliminate any part of our history that could be used against us. I told myself I was creating a new history.

"Even the townspeople who never read books were more upset over the vandalizing of the Library than over anything else I had done. Kirk was suspected by everyone now — even Anna. But still they allowed him to walk the hills and talk to Swainston.

"Accordingly, I moved into a new phase of my plan, the most thrilling part: I decided a killing or two must now be undertaken. New eras begin with killings."

HE WAS GLAD OF THE FOG as he approached Swainston's cottage at midnight. The lights were still on inside. He picked up one of the rocks that lined the path and knocked at the door.

217

The shepherd opened the door, his dogs snuffling excitedly beside him; he peered out into the fog and smiled when he saw his visitor. The smile changed to a look of surprise as the rock came down on his head. He fell. The second blow cracked the skull. His dogs were upset and licked their fallen master's face, paying no attention to his killer.

They did not interfere when he dragged the body round to the back of the cottage and propped it against the wall of the sheep pen. He wedged a flashlight between the rocks on the wall so that it shone on the dead man's face. Then, with a scalpel, he carefully cut the lips off. The blood poured thickly, the dogs whimpered and licked.

He sprayed a large circle on the gable wall, then walked back down to Carrick at a brisk pace. By the time he reached the Pharmacy, it was almost two in the morning and the fog was beginning to clear.

"What if our most malevolent, most brutal acts," said Robert Aiken, "are the ones that bring about the beneficial, progressive results? Dare we believe such a thing? I meditate on such ideas now, but that night I was too caught up in a kind of a delirium to consider matters of cause and effect.

"I had committed myself. From that moment the rock came down on the shepherd's head, I was on a dangerous and exhilarating path I had no intentions of leaving. Even though all the town now believed that Kirk must be the vandal and the killer of Swainston — even though the appointed keepers of the law were about to act — I had my own plan. I was resolved to carry it through to the end."

ON THE LAST MORNING he rose early and followed Kirk to the railway station. They stood at opposite ends of the platform for a time. When the hoot of the train sounded through the fog, he saw Kirk walk towards the edge of the platform. He himself waited till the thunder was almost on them, then he went and stood near. Kirk saw him and said something he could not hear. When the shape of the engine burst the fog apart, he felt the machine enter his heart. He pushed Kirk right into its path.

"Then, as I remember," said Robert Aiken, "in a quite methodical manner, one foot before the other, left right, left right, I marched through the fog back to Carrick."

———◆◆◆———

With those words, Aiken's monologue stopped.

I sat stunned, aware more than ever of the caustic smell that seemed to emanate from him. Then I noticed he was smiling at me. I looked closely. Yes, without any doubt, this was the old Aiken again. I could see it in his eyes. No sooner had he mouthed his last awful words, than the beast disappeared from him and the human being took possession again. For a moment, I even thought he was going to tell me it was all a joke — that he had done nothing of the sort.

That was what I hoped. But then he started to talk again, and I knew it was no joke. He began instead to plead for my understanding.

"You wonder, Maxwell, why I acted as I did? I must be honest and admit I ask myself the same thing, over and over again. I could say it was to preserve Alexander's memory or the honour of Carrick. But the truth is, I needed to do what I did. I felt as though I'd been preparing for it all my life. Even now that I know Kirk might have been my brother, it makes absolutely no difference. I haven't had the proper training for being anyone's brother."

And later he said:

"Let me explain something about my written account — the one that enticed you to Carrick in the first place. Writing it was an illuminating experience for me; it helped me to understand just how little we know about ourselves. At times I thought: the mind is like an onion, with nothing at the centre; or, at any rate, it has no more substance than a rainbow — we have to invent it each time we set out to examine it. Can we ever know ourselves well enough to know why we do anything? As for knowing other people, even those we're intimate with, even those we love, when we try to describe them, we realize what complete strangers they are. But we transform them into words anyway and pretend their minds have the same solidity as their bodies."

And later:

"When the others — Anna, Sentinel Hogg, Miss Balfour, Doctor Rankin — began to die of the poison, I went to them. It wasn't at all hard to persuade them to let me write down our story. I told them I'd make it a kind of obituary to them all, and they liked that — so long as I promised to make them interesting. Isn't that just like human beings? They wanted to be part of something coherent like those tradesmen at the festival hundreds of years ago. They even gave me suggestions: how they might look, things they might say — I took notes. I promised to make them characters in my narrative. It was like making a pleasant building out of a few heaps of bricks."

And later:

"Writing it all down wasn't easy. The words became like windows smeared with some kind of dirty oil I couldn't quite clean off; or like piranha fish — I couldn't stop them devouring whatever they got their teeth into."

And later:

"Words don't set us free, I'm afraid. They have heavy weights attached to them. Beware, Maxwell, of reading too many books. When I was young I read too much. We book readers! We lose our innocence long before anyone else. Then we crave beauty and horror and excitement, and they're in very short supply in real life."

And later:

"It's a complex knot, isn't it? The strands look as though they're all intertwined nicely, past with present, lives with lives, the living with the dead. It's a carrick bend."

And finally:

"But you, Maxwell, want to know about the poison. How am I to begin telling you about the poison?"

The thud of the soldier's boots on the stairs announced that our session was over. The air in the room was so caustic, I was struggling a little for breath. Aiken was watching me as I rose to go downstairs and he must have been afraid I wouldn't come back, for he spoke coaxingly.

"I know you're shocked, Maxwell. But you wanted the truth. Please come back tomorrow." He was smiling and wheedling. "I have to explain about the poison; that's the best part of the mystery."

The soldier interrupted; he said the physicians would be here any minute and he must prepare the room for their tests.

"Please, Maxwell. Tomorrow?" Aiken sounded a little desperate.

"All right," I said. But I couldn't look at him, I was so horrified by everything he'd told me. I stumbled down the stairs into the darkened store. The other soldier was standing inside, by the window.

"The smell in here," I said. "It's awful."

He looked puzzled. "Smell?"

Outside, it wasn't dark yet, but it was foggy as I began to walk back to the barracks. At least, I thought it was foggy; but then I realized I could see the hills quite easily — the fog was only in my mind.

I tried to think about Aiken, but I didn't know which one to think about — I'd met three Robert Aikens, all of them convincing: the cryptic observer in the narrative; then the pleasant host and conversationalist; and now this madman, this killer whose main interest seemed to be in the technical problems of writing about his crimes.

As for the others — Anna Grubach, Sentinel Hogg, Miss Balfour, Doctor Rankin — how real were they? To think they encouraged Aiken to invent their parts! Was any one of them to be trusted? Was I myself, for that matter? I was a novice all right; I was nothing but an apprentice. If only Reeve Blair were here to help me understand.

When I got to the barracks, I went to my hut. Dinner-time came and went, but I was in no mood for eating. I felt sick, so I just sat in my hut puzzling aimlessly over all I'd heard in the past few days. Around eight o'clock, I started drinking from my emergency bottle of whisky; I managed to drive the mysteries into the fog that developed in my head then I stumbled into bed and fell fast asleep.

That knocking at the door! At first I resisted it; I fitted the sound into a dream I was in the middle of, in which a hooded man drove a chisel against my skull with a hammer. Even that seemed preferable to admitting I was awake. But eventually I capitulated and opened my eyes. It wasn't even dawn yet — the outline of the window was still black. The knocking began again, so I got up — my stomach immediately reminding me I'd taken an overdose of whisky the night before to get to sleep. So nausea and I went together to the door and opened it.

The bitter cold rushed in, but the one who had been knocking, Reeve Blair, stayed outside.

"James, I just arrived from the Capital. Aiken's dead. You must come and see the body before they take it away."

I closed the door and began to dress. The news of Robert Aiken's death didn't shock me perhaps because I was feeling too absorbed in myself and my hungover condition. If I thought anything, it was that Aiken might have enjoyed the drama of this early morning knocking on the door to announce his death. It was just the kind of thing he might have planned.

Reeve Blair waited for me at the mess-hut while I drank a cup of black coffee that didn't help me much; then we set out together for the town. The dawn was just a slit in the eastern sky and the air was frigid. Even the stars were shrivelled.

After a silent walk, we arrived in Carrick. I could see no guards around the Green except for the three figures on the Monument, ever alert, but blind.

Outside the Pharmacy a balloon of smoke was having trouble separating itself from a parked ambulance's tail pipe. A soldier opened the Pharmacy door for us and we stepped into the warm interior. My nose was immediately on the defensive, but no other smell assailed it this time than the traditional odours of a pharmacy in a small town in the hills. Reeve Blair led the way to the rear and up the familiar, worn stairs.

In the upper room, men in various uniforms were huddled in consultation, talking quietly. They nodded to the Reeve as we passed them and went into Aiken's bedroom. A photographer was busy there, making his still lifes of the dead.

"Give us a few minutes alone," the Reeve said.

The photographer joined the others in the living-room, leaving three of us: me, Reeve Blair and the naked corpse of Aiken on the bed.

I made myself look at him, or it. The eyes were closed lightly, and the lips were apart. The face displayed that surrender of the will to live that marks the faces of the dead. As for the rest of the body, it had turned waxy grey.

But it was not just to see a dead body Reeve Blair had brought me here at this hour of the morning. Aiken's torso was covered in handwriting, done in faint black ink, diluted by his dying sweat.

"Go ahead," said the Reeve. "It's for you."

Aiken had apparently made a final manuscript of his body. His left side between shoulder and hip was the top of the page, the right side between shoulder and hip was the bottom; words covered all of it except where he had drawn little circles around the territory of the nipples and the navel; the right margin was marked by a line above the straggle of grey pubic hair that surrounded his shrunken genitals. The near right of his torso must have been awkward for him to reach and the writing there was more clumsy.

"Read it," said the Reeve.

I leaned over, a little apprehensively, but there was no trace of that acrid smell. Aiken's last communication began at the tip of the left shoulder:

Maxwell:

I write this at 3 A.M. The fever has struck and I know my time is running out — I hereby cancel our interview in the morning! This is my last page, so I must make every word count: a good lesson for an apprentice journalist to learn.

The last mysteries at Carrick are these: why did I poison the others? why did I poison myself? I would have told you the answers at our next appointment, but now you'll just have to work them out for yourself.

I feel very feverish now. Sorry I didn't get to know you better.

Aiken takes his bow.

Good-night.

The writing was clumsy, but the message fitted the space perfectly; the last word, "Good-night," was almost at the back of the solar plexus. I read and re-read while Reeve Blair leafed through some pieces of paper that were lying beside the bed.

"Rough notes," he said. "Would you believe it? He actually planned out exactly what he could write in the space available. Would you like to glance at them? I wonder if he made any last minute changes."

I looked at him, but he did not seem to be joking.

All that afternoon, back at the barracks, Reeve Blair listened to the tapes I'd made of my interviews with Robert Aiken. His face was quite inscrutable for much of them, though he raised his eyebrows once or twice. Especially at the part where Aiken described his discovery that Kirk might be his brother. As for Aiken's confession to the acts of vandalism and to the murders of Swainston and Kirk, he listened intently; and when he did make a comment at the end, it wasn't quite what I'd expected.

"You did a very good job, James," he said. "You inspired him."

In retrospect, that should have made me suspicious, but I took it as flattery and didn't pursue it. In the hour that was left, I continued my packing as we talked. I mentioned Anna Grubach again. I said I was sorry I'd never see her again — and that made me think of Reeve Blair's own youthful romance with the older woman. "Did you ever see her again?" I asked. "I mean Veronica."

"That's one loose end I don't mind tying up for you, James," he said. "Yes, I did see her again. Just five years ago. I was working on a case in the South, so I drove over to where she lived. She'd moved by then to another town along the coast. I thought she wouldn't object to seeing me, just to reminisce about the old days."

REEVE BLAIRS FIRST LOVE (CONT.)

(transcribed from tape and condensed by me, James Maxwell)

She lived in a little house not far from the beach, and it was another windy, grey day. He was looking for a place to park when he saw her, coming along the street. She looked as wonderful as ever — her face hadn't aged at all after almost twenty-five years. He parked and ran after her, shouting:

"Veronica! Veronica!"

She turned and waited for him. When he reached her, he saw she looked puzzled.

"Veronica!" he said. "Don't you remember me?" He was jubilant, he wanted to take her in his arms — he was in love with her still!

"I'm not Veronica," she said. "She's my mother. Do you want to come in and see her? She's very sick."

He didn't know what to say. Veronica's daughter had the same black hair, the same cheek-bones, the same quick eyes as her mother. She was about the same age as himself.

He said he'd made a mistake and without waiting for her questions, he went back to his car, opened the door and sat inside. He looked at his reflection in the rear mirror — a man in his forties with grey hair, hollow cheeks and lines at his eyes. He was aware he might still have got out of the car and gone to the house with Veronica's daughter. But he didn't. He told himself the visit was a bad idea. He put the car in gear and drove away without looking back.

———————◆●◆———————

"You see, James, for years I'd loved the image of a Veronica who never aged. I grew older myself till I caught up with that image When I saw it embodied in Veronica's daughter, I still loved it and desired it. That was what I'd come to see — not some old woman." His voice was quiet and controlled as ever. "When I realized what was going through my mind, I felt like a traitor. I couldn't help remembering what

Veronica had said about love; it was like a prophecy that had come to pass. That's what I was thinking about as I drove away."

A soldier came to the hut just then to tell me the jeep that was to take me back to the Capital had arrived; so I didn't have time to ask Reeve Blair any more about himself and Veronica. I quickly packed my few remaining possessions into my bag: my tape-recorder and my notes; and, on top, my copy of Aiken's narrative (I washed my hands afterwards — that peculiar smell clung to everything). Then I walked with the Reeve to the barracks gate where the jeep was waiting. We shook hands.

"I'll see you again," I said.

"You can be sure of it," he said. He handed me an envelope. "Here's a souvenir of Carrick."

I climbed into the rear of the jeep; its camouflage served no purpose in the dark. The Reeve was standing in the doorway of the mess-hall as we left. I waved goodbye, and the jeep made its way out of the barracks and down into the town.

Passing through Carrick, I took a last look around. The boards over the windows in Anna's store glistened with rain. There was no light in the upper room of the Pharmacy. A truck stood outside the Library, half-filled with books destined for incineration. The doors and windows of the Keep and The Stag were barred. In the midst of all stood the Monument, its three blind figures guarding a town whose inhabitants they would no longer need eyes to see.

With Carrick behind us, the jeep speeded up, quarrelling its way through the gears up the steep hill of the northern route. Far to the west, a wedge of violet was jammed between the horizon and the black sky. I put my hand in my pocket and felt the smooth envelope Reeve Craig had given me. I switched on the overhead map-light and opened the envelope. In it was a close-up photograph of Aiken's corpse — the message on it was quite legible.

What a death-bed testament! I thought. How bizarre that Robert Aiken should play such games right to the last moment of his life — as though his obsession with words, with writing them down, was nothing more than an unrecognized symptom of the poison in him.

I slid the photo back into the envelope. I was tired after my long day and from the heat of the jeep. Through the window I could see, several miles away to the east, the Cairn looming darker than the darkness of the night, and I thought of the murder that had been committed so crazily there, so long ago.

How fearful it must have been for those prisoners as they heard the groaning of the wooden props that held up the mountain above them and felt the shower of rock-chips on their bare flesh. I imagine them straightening their backs, some of them leaning on their picks. They look at each other. Silence. Silence. Silence. They begin to breathe again, deeply, they bend again to hack and hew at the jagged seam. But now pitch-blackness swallows the string of light-bulbs above and behind them. Only the glow of fifteen helmet-lamps traces the fragility of the ribcages of shirtless bodies. The white of their eyes becomes a symbol.

And now they hear thunder deep in the earth where

there can be no thunder. The tunnel vibrates around them — fifteen men waiting, some of them still holding onto their picks, not knowing what else to do.

The roar and the monster that utters it arrive together and shatter their pale bodies. The jagged edges they have created now become their impalers. Then utter silence.

The jeep bumped over a pothole and shook those images out of my mind. I wiped the steaming window. To the west, the violet hour had passed and night was supreme. In the headlamps of the jeep, the road hissed steadily northwards. Two hours from now we would descend from the Uplands, and this road would converge with another, and would be joined by more and more branch roads and subsidiary roads, and eventually we would enter a maze of highways and by-passes, and slink anonymously once more into the great insoluble knot of the Capital.

4

---

*This world lacks so much that,
if one more thing went missing, there
would not be any room for it.*

MACEDONIO FERNANDEZ

Well, there you have the facts: Robert Aiken's written narrative, my transcriptions of the interviews in Carrick, my conversations with Reeve Blair and my reactions on seeing Aiken's body that cold morning in March, all those years ago. My series of articles on Carrick was published in newspapers throughout the Island — you may have read them at the time. On the strength of their success, I abandoned my university studies and began to work full time for *The Voice*. I didn't have to cover Council meetings any more, and my copy was usually left unedited.

Then a publisher in the Capital suggested I write a retrospective, in-depth book on the happenings at Carrick, and I agreed. I was deeply thrilled at the idea of being a real author.

I took the whole thing very seriously. I dug out all my old notes and spent most of my spare time for twelve months checking out everything that could be verified from independent sources. The incident at the Mord River Bridge, for example. I discovered three separate

accounts by eye-witnesses, all saying they'd seen the soldiers plunge into the river much as in the pamphlet I'd
read in Carrick.

As for the drowning of the prisoners of war from Camp
Zero: I spent weeks in the Regional Archives before I
unearthed the only remaining copy of the report of the
Commission of Inquiry. It was brief and categorical: a
flash-explosion of subterranean gases had occurred at the
Carrick Mine and had fractured a layer of rock, thus
allowing water from the St Giles Pond to pour into the
lower galleries; no human intervention could have made
any difference.

The report also confirmed Doctor Rankin's claim
about the chronology of events. In fact, the commissioners made an issue of it. They stated clearly that the
prisoners in the Mine died a full twenty-four hours before
anyone in Carrick knew about that other drowning (i.e.
of the Carrick men at the Mord River Bridge). Therefore, they said, there was absolutely no basis for suspect-
ing that the prisoners had been deliberately killed as an
act of vengeance by the townspeople of Carrick.

One item was missing from the copy of the report: a
list of the prisoners' names was supposed to be appended;
but I could see no sign of it. I asked the archivist and she
said it had probably been misplaced in the course of re-
arranging the archives over the years. She had no doubt
it would turn up some day — probably by accident.

As part of my research, I also thought it might be wise
to look into Kirk's background, so I took a trip to the
Colony. That was the first time I ever left the Island. I
went by ship, the way exiles had gone for centuries to

settle the Colony. It was quite an experience to cross that great waste of ocean; but even more incredible for me was the journey up the Colony's main river; we'd actually been inside the land mass a thousand miles before the river narrowed enough to see the banks on either side with their great evergreen forests.

Our ship anchored at one of the lake ports and from there I took a train to visit the research station where Kirk had been based. I met the head of his department, a tall, pleasant man with a cast in his eye, who seemed able to look in two directions at once like a rabbit. He said he'd always admired Kirk's work, but didn't know him well personally. Some of Kirk's colleagues said he'd been a loner and discouraged friendship. But they'd all been looking forward to the results of his research at Carrick.

I spent the next few weeks pleasantly wandering around the Interlake area half-sightseeing, half-researching. At the provincial capital, I went to the Hall of Records and checked on Kirk's mother. That was useful. She was listed as "Martha Kirk" on her entry into the Colony as a refugee, but a handwritten note by the registrar at the time indicated that "Kirk" was not her original name — it was one that was allocated to her when she landed.

I spoke to one of the Assistant Recorders about this. He said it had been a very common practice at that time to give easily spelt names to exiles from the Continent. Since most of them had no papers, especially during the War, there would be no way now of finding out what her real name was — unless it was on Kirk's birth certificate.

The Assistant was very helpful. He searched among various file catalogues and eventually found the registration of Kirk's birth. But again, "Martha Kirk" was listed as his mother's name. In the space for the father's name, there was a question mark.

After a month, I came back home to the Island, knowing little more than when I'd left. I was more sure than ever that ultimately everything rested on the credibility of Anna and Sentinel Hogg and Miss Balfour and Doctor Rankin and Aiken himself — all of them dead now and, therefore, not to be cross-examined.

I should mention that I *did* manage to find the relatives of some of those who'd died in Carrick. The grown-up daughter of Kennedy, for example: she was a squat, black-haired woman, a cakemaker with a little store on the High Street in the Capital. She was friendly enough to me at the beginning when she thought I was a customer and wanted to order a cake. But when I told her I would like to ask her some questions about Carrick and her father, she became very hostile.

"Mind your own business," she said. "Get out of my shop and don't come back."

I won't detail my visits to other relatives of the dead townspeople; that incident with Kennedy's daughter pretty well sums up the treatment I received from them all. Their attitude didn't really surprise me.

When I'd exhausted the useful possibilities of further research, I sat down and began to write my book — *The Beast of Carrick* — much as you've read it to this point. In my final chapter, written with whatever advantages hindsight is supposed to bring, I tried to fit the pieces together. No easy matter. Of the several mysteries at Carrick, some seemed more baffling than others. Why, after trying to incriminate Kirk in his written account, did Aiken confess his own guilt to me during the interviews? Why did he poison the whole population? Why (this, for me, was most puzzling of all) did none of the townspeople condemn him?

In that last chapter of my book, I argued that perhaps it was futile to try and find reasoned explanations for a madman's actions and motivations. Aiken was capable of being very human, even likeable, but he was also his father's son. The world of his mind was a nightmare, and not amenable to exploration by those of us who regard ourselves as sane. I referred to Anna Grubach's characterization of Aiken: "He's always been like a stick in water. Is he bent, or is he not?"

And I concluded Robert Aiken was indeed bent.

So at the end of that year, a final draft of *The Beast* was almost finished. I didn't regret the time I'd spent on it. To have arrived at a perspective on the events at Carrick and to have put it down on paper at last was a relief. I planned to finish my revisions and hand the manuscript over to my publisher.

Then I'd destroy my wad of Carrick files, and get on with my life.

That was my plan.

It was a good plan, a very good plan, and like many good plans it didn't last long. I was sitting at my office desk just a couple of afternoons after I'd made it. I was working at final revisions to *The Beast*, gazing out of my window at the Necropolis from time to time. I was wondering perhaps if only death finally can impose order on the chaos of existence. Anyway, just at that moment, the phone rang.

"James. This is Reeve Blair."

"Reeve Blair!" I hadn't heard from him for months. "What can I do for you?" I know I sounded cheerful, carefree. He didn't answer right away and I didn't like that. Ever since my exposure to Carrick I suppose I'd become less of a simpleton than I once was, a little more aware of complexities. So that pause on the other end of the phone put me on guard.

"Perhaps, James, it's more a case of what I can do for you." His voice was gentle. "How's your book going?"

"Quite well. I hope it'll be fairly definitive. My research has been useful, I think." My voice didn't sound convincing. "I'm in the throes of the final revision, right now. But please. What's wrong?"

"I regret to say that you're not in possession of all the facts. There have been certain developments." In spite of his soft, unhurried voice, those dry, bureaucratic phrases were chilling. "Perhaps we could meet today, James? Yes. I think we should meet today."

At three o'clock, as I walked to the Old Town, a cool wind from the Firth and a squall of rain accompanied me. When I reached The Last Minstrel I pushed the door open and went inside. I knew the bar well, with its dusty plastic claymores and targes on top of a tartan wallpaper that was bleary from layers of smoke. Often the junior reporters from *The Voice* would meet there for a drink at night. But now the clientele consisted of the usual handful of gloomy portraits and a handful of even gloomier customers. Reeve Blair, sitting in one of the dimly lit corners, fitted the place well. Certainly, on the outside he was ascetic looking enough, with his thin face and closely cropped grey hair. He rose and shook hands with me.

"Sit down, James. I've ordered a drink for you." We made some small talk till my drink arrived. We drank each other's health then I went straight to the point.

"Reeve Blair, don't keep me in suspense. You may as well tell me what you think I ought to know. May I use my tape-recorder?"

He nodded, I switched it on and he, in his confiding way, began to tell me what he had learnt.

"Atkinson," he said, lassoing the word to one corner of his mouth. "Atkinson was the man responsible."

Atkinson was a member of the Public Safety Council, and had been conducting yet another test in Carrick. All signs of the poison had disappeared so the council was beginning to consider whether the area should be opened up again for fishing.

The afternoon of the test was a rainy one, of course. Atkinson was up among the hills, inspecting the area around the St Giles Pond. As he passed the Monolith on the south side, he saw, for the first time, the niches cut into it. He was curious, so he began climbing, very carefully, for the steps were worn and covered with moss.

He slithered over the rim and almost rolled into a shallow puddle that filled most of the hollow on top. He immediately saw, half-immersed in the puddle, a black box with a leather shoulder strap. He leaned over and fished the box out. It was bound shut with a piece of very wet rope. He took out his penknife and cut the rope, but the box still wouldn't open. He prised at the lock till it broke off, then he lifted the lid.

One brief look at the contents of the box convinced Atkinson he'd found something significant. He tied the rope round the box again, threw it over the edge of the Monolith and climbed down after it. Then he carried it back quickly to Carrick.

After Reeve Blair told me about Atkinson's discovery, we had a long conversation — one that was momentous for me. In what follows, I've transcribed most of that conversation verbatim because of its significance. I've omitted most of my reactions to what Reeve Blair said; but it's easy to imagine them — bewilderment, disappointment and, first and foremost, embarrassment at my own pathetic attempt to explain the Carrick mysteries.

THE DIALOGUE AT THE LAST MINSTREL

BLAIR (*reaches into the inside pocket of his jacket and brings out an envelope*): Atkinson has a very inquiring mind. A hundred other men searched all over that area and not one of them thought of climbing the Monolith. That black box Atkinson found had two items of interest in it; one of them is in this envelope.

MAXWELL: Don't tell me it's another note.

BLAIR: If you can bear it. (*He opens the envelope and hands Maxwell a piece of yellow notepaper; it is lined, perforated along one edge.*)

MAXWELL (*reading aloud*):

To the finder:

I, the undersigned, confess to damaging the Monument, and the graveyard, and the Library at Carrick. But I did not kill Adam Swainston. I was with him in his cottage when he suffered a stroke and fell down dead. I didn't report it, because I was already under suspicion.

My only regret is the unhappiness I've brought to Anna Grubach. I have no intention of humiliating her, or myself, any longer.

Certain other objects can be found at the site of Camp Zero.

Martin Kirk

BLAIR (*to Maxwell, still staring at the paper*): It's in Kirk's handwriting. Why he left it in the box on the Monolith I don't know — it might never have been found. You'll notice he claims *he* was responsible for the vandalism and that Swainston died a natural death.

MAXWELL: But Aiken said . . .

BLAIR: Wait till you hear the rest, James. I said there were two things in the box. Here's the other. (*He reaches into his jacket again and this time brings out an off-white handkerchief with a solid object wrapped in it. He puts it carefully on the table in front of Maxwell and peels away the cloth. In the centre of the handkerchief lies a cloven hoof and a few inches of sheep's hock with grey wool still intact; jagged sinews and bone protrude from the end.*) You remember the sheep that was half-buried in the graveyard? When we dug it up, we discovered one of its hoofs had been cut off at the first joint. This is it. Aiken told you he threw the sheep in the grave, but he didn't say anything about cutting off the hoof. Only the real vandal knew that.

MAXWELL: But it's only one detail . . .

BLAIR: Ah, but there's more. On the basis of Kirk's note, we sent a squad to search the site of Camp Zero. They didn't have to look for long. They found a canvas bag under some bracken. Inside it was the plaque from the Monument together with some small brass name-plates from gravestones. There was a book from the section of the Library that was ruined. And there were other things too: some cans of red spray-paint, chisels, tubes of lip-stick, an axe and various other tools.

MAXWELL (*about to say something*): I . . . I see.

BLAIR: As for the death of Swainston: who knows? Maybe he was already dead when Aiken arrived. It's a matter of Aiken's credibility, and that isn't very strong, is it? Maybe he did mutilate the body, but can we believe him when he says he killed Swainston? For that matter, can we believe him when he says he pushed Kirk in front of the train? For all we know, Kirk may have fallen. Or jumped. It's very possible, isn't it? Perhaps that's what the last words of the note mean.

MAXWELL: I suppose so.

BLAIR (*sitting slightly stooped, sipping from his glass of whisky with two hands, as though it were a chalice*): I could go on suggesting other variations — I'm sure you can see them yourself, James. Isn't it strange how in these Carrick mysteries one possibility melts into another. Like one of those medieval manuscripts where you rub away one text and find another underneath. And maybe even another, and another. Here's what I'm getting at and I'd like you to consider it: An awful thing did happen in Carrick years ago during the War, there's no denying that. Those prisoners of war were drowned. That's a fact. Was it murder? If we can believe Anna Grubach, Sentinel Hogg, Miss Balfour and Doctor Rankin, it certainly was. But even if it was, there's nothing we can do about it now. So what about these more recent events — the ones that you and I investigated last year? The time has come, James, for us to ask ourselves a very important question: Aside from some nasty acts of vandalism, aside from the mutilation of a corpse — *what if there really was no great crime committed in Carrick last year?*

MAXWELL: I don't understand.

BLAIR (*sets his glass down on the table beside the sheep's hoof*): I'll put it to you straight: perhaps what we're facing here may be a great *mystery*; but it may be a mystery with no great *crime* to match it.

MAXWELL (*suddenly excited*): Hold everything, Reeve Blair! You're forgetting about the most important thing of all! The poison! Aiken may have been a liar, but what about the poison? There's no arguing about that. Someone poisoned all those people. It doesn't matter whether it was Aiken or Kirk or someone else. The fact remains, there *was* a great crime at Carrick. Someone in Carrick was a mass-murderer.

BLAIR (*shaking his head slowly*): No. I'm afraid not, James. Neither Aiken nor Kirk nor anyone else was the poisoner. I met with the Chief Medical Officer just this morning. It was after I spoke to him I knew I must get in touch with you.

The Chief Medical Officer prospered on human misery, thought Reeve Blair. His belly seemed even bigger than when they'd last met, as though a new, larger sized balloon had been squeezed under his shirt front. Yet he was as neat and well tailored as ever, the parting in his oily hair precise as an incision. This table they were sitting at was right in the middle of the Chief Medical Officer's favourite restaurant; the lunch-time clientele at tables all around seemed as prosperous as Reeve Blair's host. The Reeve felt unkempt and out of place.

The Chief Medical Officer was delivering a brief lecture to him and was impatient; he wanted to get on with ordering his meal.

"What alerted our people — even though it was a false alert — was the presence of out-of-season flies and wasps at Carrick. They followed the trail of the wasps into a narrow hole in the side of the Cairn. That hole was connected to a series of natural caverns which in turn ran deeper still, hundreds of feet down to the galleries of the old St Giles Mine.

"There you have it, Blair! Another mystery solved for you! It was the heat deep below the earth that kept the insects alive through the winter.

"Now our people were always suspicious of the wasps — they thought perhaps the poison had been transmitted through their stings — you know nearly everybody in Carrick had been stung.

"Well, they were wrong about that. But it was while they were down there examining the water in the flooded galleries that — BINGO!" — the Chief Medical Officer banged the table loudly with his fist, too loudly the Reeve thought — "they found the source of the poison. The water! The water down there was completely contaminated. They could tell even by looking at it. Back in the lab, they analysed it. It was full of bacteria that were mutations of *suppurata gravissima*. It's a bacterium that develops in decaying animal matter — it's very common in wet tropical regions after flooding or landslides where a lot of dead animals are left to rot. In Carrick, over a long period of years, the combination of the decayed bodies of the drowned prisoners together with the underground heat brought about a similar phenomenon. A particularly virulent strain of it seems to have found its way into the moorland streams that supply the drinking water. It only lasted for a few weeks then died out. We've snuffed it out now."

He reached for the menu.

"I hope all of this technical stuff isn't too difficult for you, Blair. The long and short of it is, a natural agent killed all those people. The mass-murderer you've been looking for in Carrick has been loose around the world for millenia and will get us all in the end. I refer, of course, to nature."

The Chief Medical Officer opened the menu and turned his attention to choosing the entrées.

THE DIALOGUE AT THE LAST MINSTREL (CONT.)

BLAIR: Robert Aiken and the people of Carrick didn't know the poison was natural. After a while they were sure someone had poisoned them: it fitted the pattern of violence on violence. We thought so too. Aiken had seen Kirk at the water source with his powders and was convinced he was the poisoner. But our investigators knew all about Aiken and his herbs and roots and elixirs. When he seemed to be the only one who wasn't poisoned, they were sure he was the poisoner. And really, all along, there never was a poisoner — just a possible case of poetic justice.
MAXWELL: (*attempts to laugh*)
BLAIR: So nothing was as it seemed. Kirk was the vandal and perhaps killed himself; Swainston may have died due to a stroke; and the poison that killed all the other townspeople was quite natural. In other words, James, it looks as though Robert Aiken was innocent. He confessed to all these crimes — even the murder of his friends — and we know now he did nothing of the sort. The mystery we're left with is this: Why did he confess?

MAXWELL (*looking desperate or hopeful*): Is it possible that he really was trying to make amends for his father's crime by taking the blame? You know, trying to correct history?

BLAIR: You may be right. You probably understood these people much better than I did. I wonder, though. Is it possible that when they thought Kirk had managed to poison them all, they decided not to allow a stranger the credit for it? In fact, they didn't want him to have the credit for anything, not even the vandalism. They wanted one of their own, a Carrick man, to have all the credit — and Robert Aiken was happy to oblige.

MAXWELL: Why did he bother writing his account, and having me brought here, and all the rest of it? When you charged him, why didn't he confess right away if that's what he wanted.

BLAIR: I have a feeling he wanted much more than that. I believe he wanted to contrive a great mystery. He certainly succeeded in giving . . .

My tape ran out at that point, but I remember what followed well enough. Reeve Blair's use of the word "credit" had sounded so odd I thought he must be joking. But I could see no hint of a smile. After that I sat silently — silent with dismay — considering the implications of his theory.

But in due course, whisky oiled the machinery of my mouth, and I stayed with Reeve Blair for several hours in The Last Minstrel that day discussing the mysteries at

Carrick from this angle and that, considering such matters as guilt, innocence, doubt and certainty.

"Reeve Blair, did you yourself believe Aiken was guilty when you charged him? I mean, did you think he was a vandal and a killer?"

"You know I never rush to conclusions, James. I could see he *wanted* to be charged, so I obliged him."

I knew him well enough by now not to think his answer strange. I continued: "If the others were in on it too all along, can we believe anything they said?"

"You're thinking well, James." He nodded his head. "That too must be considered."

"Was it all lies, then?"

"I think in this case the truth may be impossible to separate from the lies. When a story rings true and we've no way of discounting it, why shouldn't we believe it? Didn't Aiken's father say something like that about the old sailor at the festival?"

"Yes. 'A man's life may be a lie, and his stories may be the absolute truth.'" I thought about that for a moment before the irony of it struck me. "At least, that's what Aiken *said* his father said!"

When it was time for him to leave, Reeve Blair shook my hand.

"I know the people of Carrick weren't fond of Southerners," he said. "But I must confess I found them fascinating."

"Reeve Blair," I said (I'd had much too much to drink by then), "I don't think you're nearly as unlike them as they thought." He looked at me even more sternly than usual, but I believe that was only to hide his pleasure at my comment. The whisky in me made me bolder still. "By the way," I said. "That smell I kept noticing in Carrick. Did you smell it?"

The austerity of his face softened slightly.

"Ah, the smell. Well done, James. I knew I'd picked the right man for the job." Then before he turned away to leave, he said, almost in a whisper: "I've trained myself in the small mysteries all my life. I never thought I'd be fortunate enough to stumble upon a great one — a *mysterium mysteriorum*. Thank you, James Maxwell, for your participation in it with me."

I didn't publish my book. Not because my theories about Carrick and Aiken had been hopelessly wrong. I was young enough to get over that blow and I set about making extensive revisions. I even sent a copy of the manuscript to Reeve Blair. He read it and sent it back with a note in his own precise handwriting.

James:

I only gave it a brief glance. Comments:

(1) Your transcriptions and condensations of the Carrick interviews were very selective: I'm left wondering why you chose the more sensational parts and omitted others? Is it wise to editorialize evidence? Need I remind you of your own views on editors?

(2) I'd be grateful if you'd cut me (i.e. the character "Reeve Blair") out of the finished work altogether.

(3) I'm afraid you made no sense of my "lecture" on Criminal Theory.

Sorry. I know you mean to be kind.

Blair

Not even the implications of that note discouraged me. No, what put a stop to my plans for publishing *The Beast* was a conversation I had with my own father. He told me something that made me feel I'd be better just to drop the whole project.

We were sitting by the fireplace in the house where I was born and he was puffing at his pipe. The smell of his tobacco smoke always brought on a great sense of nostalgia for childhood in me. I'd taken to visiting him often after the death of my mother, whom we'd both loved very much. He'd begun to look suddenly older, as though age had been hiding in him while my mother was alive and had decided it was now safe to come out. I'd been talking to him about my book and my plans for re-writing it.

"This pharmacist from Carrick," he said, "this Aiken. Is there any chance he's related to us?"

"What?" I almost choked, and not from the pipe smoke.

"An aunt of mine — she'd be your great-aunt — ran away from home with some professional man from the Uplands. I can't remember whether he was a dentist or a pharmacist — something like that. I was only five or six at the time. I have the impression she was a sort of black sheep. She didn't keep in touch with any of the family, so that's all I know about her."

"Father! Why didn't you mention this before?"

"It just crossed my mind while you were talking," he said. "Anyway, it's not very likely, is it? But you could check it out if you wanted."

I would sooner have swallowed a toad. I was appalled at the very idea. Nor could I help remembering that Aiken had joked about how much I looked like him. And some of the others had stared at me when they first saw me. What if Aiken was actually aware of this possible relationship between the two of us, and that was why he asked for me? What if Anna and Sentinel Hogg and Miss Balfour and Doctor Rankin knew it too? What if that was the only reason they agreed to talk to me? What if Reeve Blair knew — and of course didn't say anything! What if Aiken and Kirk and I were relatives?

What if! What if! What if!

The thought of living in a world so patterned, so contrived — a world *without mystery* — horrified me. It was even worse than Anna Grubach's vision of a motiveless, plotless universe. I decided right then I didn't want to know more. I preferred my ignorance.

5

---•◦•---

If you don't know you don't know,
you think you know;
if you don't know you know,
you think you don't know.

R.D. LAING

All of that was such a long time ago.

Reeve Blair and I remained great friends (in spite of his unenthusiastic review of my manuscript!) till his death. That was a long time ago, too. I stood at his burial in the Necropolis one very rainy day. Among the mourners (mainly his fellow-reeves and other police officials, none of whom seemed very mournful), I saw his sister. I'd never met her, but he'd often mentioned her. She was as tall as he was, thin and reserved looking. She wore a black coat and hat, but no veil over her grey hair. At the end of the burial, I introduced myself and said how sorry I was. She thanked me.

"We were separated as children, you know," she said. "He searched for me later and found me, and he was always kind to me. But we weren't much alike." I found that amusing; even her lips had the same quirk as his, gathering the words into one corner before releasing them. "I wanted security in my life. But that wasn't for him. He said he didn't want to know the ways of the world by heart; he was going to enjoy the mysteries. He was in love with his mysteries." She shook my hand and walked away to the waiting limousine.

Earlier tonight, I attended one of those civic banquets; this time, I myself sat at the head table and gave one of the boring speeches. As usual, these affairs get me to thinking again about Carrick (I've made many efforts over the years to write one final draft of *The Beast* — even though I should know better and in spite of all my good resolutions). When I got home I went to my study and took out that old copy of Robert Aiken's narrative that had accompanied me to Carrick.

It was as enigmatic as ever and so was its author. I believe now that Anna Grubach (how beautiful she still seems to me) was right when she spoke about the futility of searching for cause and effect. Hindsight, I think, frequently makes sense of things past by assigning causes for them that are fictitious or quite superficial.

As I write this, it's just after midnight.

I'm quite old myself now, with a wife, grown-up children and a grandchild. My wife and I are still in love (a miracle, surely). When we first met, her green eyes reminded me of Anna Grubach — that was what attracted me to her, though I never told her so. I once showed her my manuscript of *The Beast*; she tried to read it, but couldn't finish it.

"I'd rather read about people like ourselves who're relatively happy and relatively normal," she said.

"Really James, why would you even want to write about people like these?"

At one time, I might have said for money, or for fame. That week in Carrick (I might have said) was the most interesting thing that has ever happened to me; and the people I met there were the most interesting people I have ever met. I might even have asked — more honestly — why would I write about lives like ours that are so ordinary, so dull?

But of course I didn't put such a question to someone I love who loves me and has tolerated me for so many years. Besides, the fact is, I no longer know *why* I wrote it, or even *what it's about*. All I know is that I *did* write it at a certain time in my life, and it's important to me because of that. Like a man seeing a figure on the far side of a river, and not wanting to let it out of sight because in some odd, tangible way it's himself when he was young.

I'm editor of *The Voice* now, and I'm regarded as "a prominent citizen" of the Capital, indeed of this entire Island (or at least the Northern part). That prominence hasn't stopped me from suffering two minor heart attacks in the last year, however. My doctor has warned me the third might not be so minor. In fact, he said, it might be fatal.

It's hard for me to accept the thought of my own death, though I'm quite used to the idea that others must die. In that regard, I feel just as immature as I was when I was an apprentice. Wisdom and resignation come too late, if ever, to some of us.

Wouldn't a wise man, for example, be able to resist bending over Aiken's stained and wrinkled narrative, resist sniffing at it? As I do now. I can smell nothing strange, only fusty paper. Does that mean it is no longer contaminated? Or does it mean that I have joined all those others who didn't seem to notice that sour smell a long time ago in Carrick?

I remember something Reeve Blair said to me in an oracular moment shortly before he died:

"James," he said, "the truly wise are those who become just wise enough to hold on to their innocence."

When I have understood that fully, will I at last have completed my apprenticeship?

Certum quia impossibile